THE TRAIN TO ESTELLINE

"This one will steal your heart and make you glad to be alive. . . . *The Train* provides a thoroughly enjoyable, entirely too brief ride backward in time."
—*Valley Morning Star* (Harlingen, Texas)

"Stylish, spare, and swiftly paced, *The Train to Estelline* spotlights a year in the life of a youthful and spirited pioneer teacher who sets out at the turn of the century to seek 'a wider world.' The one she finds exceeds her dreams and expands her life. . . . Warm and moving."
—*Sherman Democrat*

"A clear view of rural West Texas in 1912. Illness, birth, death are soon very real to Lucy, and she finds herself redefining her moral values, teaching goals, and her own needs for personal fulfillment. . . . Wood doesn't get on a soapbox. She's too subtle and too skillful for that. Her story, simply, entertainingly, effectively related, speaks for itself."
—*The Arlington Daily News*

"I ran it through three generations of readers—mother, wife, and child—and unanimously they read it with pleasure and commented with applause. Then I read it—this story of a young country-school teacher in the Texas Panhandle of 1911—and found it rich, and loving and real, and a true gripper, hard to put down once you started reading."
—*The Nacogdoches, Texas, Daily Sentinel*

"A charming, compelling story."
—Martina Horner, President, Radcliffe College

THE TRAIN TO ESTELLINE

Jane Roberts Wood

LAUREL

A LAUREL TRADE PAPERBACK
Published by
Dell Publishing
a division of
The Bantam Doubleday Dell Publishing Group, Inc.
1 Dag Hammarskjold Plaza
New York, New York 10017

Reprinted by arrangement with Ellen C. Temple, Publisher

Laurel ® TM 674623, Dell Publishing, a division of the Bantam Doubleday Dell Publishing Group, Inc.

ISBN: 0-440-50033-8

Printed in the United States of America

Published simultaneously in Canada

July 1988

10 9 8 7 6 5 4 3 2 1

W

To BETTY PARSONS DOOLEY

My twin sister

July 25, 1911
Bonham, Texas

Mr. Robert Sully
Box 48
White Star, Texas
Dear Sir:

I am applying for the teaching position you advertised in the Fort Worth Star-Telegram on July 23, 1911.

I am a graduate of Bonham High School and of Kitty Quay Normal, and, as such, I am qualified to teach all grades. I am unmarried, attend church, and have no bad habits. I will be eighteen before Christmas.

The teaching of twelve to fifteen students in grades one through ten offers a challenge I believe I can meet.

Enclosed is a copy of my school record and three letters of recommendation.

Sincerely,
Lucinda Eliza Richards

August 13, 1911
Bonham, Texas

Dear Mr. Sully,

I am pleased to accept the position in the White Star school for the coming year. The salary offer of forty-two dollars per month along with room and board is quite satisfactory.

I will be on the train to Estelline September 1, and I look forward to meeting you then.

Sincerely,
Lucy Eliza Richards

August 17, 1911
Bonham, Texas

Dear Diary,

I have a job! I sing the words. My heart dances them. The leaves on the magnolia tree outside my window whisper them. Lucy has a job. No. Miss Lucinda Eliza Richards has a position!

I am going to teach on a ranch in West Texas. If Mama knew how happy I am to be leaving, how relieved, it would just about break her heart. But I am tired of her sad face and of Aunt Catherine's holier-than-thouness, and all Lillian ever talks about is dumplings and bedroom curtains. I have longed for a wider world, a great adventure. And now it's here.

I'm so happy I can hardly breathe.

Love,
Lucy

August 30, 1911
On the Texas and Pacific

Dear Mama,

When Katie began to cry, there we were, all of us a muddled mess, crying and hugging and kissing each other. Only George, now the man in the family, was dry-eyed.

Just as he promised, Mr. Walker is taking good care of me. From the time he called out, "All aboard," until now, I have not been out of his sight a minute. Whether he is taking up tickets or helping a passenger off the train, he always has one eye on me.

I wish my going away had not come so soon after Papa's death, but I am, after all, seventeen, and it is time for me to make my way in the world. Your courage provides the strength I need to leave my dear family at this time. We will stay very near each other as our letters go back and forth, weaving a web of closeness between us.

Your loving,
Lucy

August 30, 1911
Aboard the Fort Worth and Denver

Dearest Aunt Catherine,

Although you were unable to come to the station to see me off, I felt your presence. At seven o'clock, the train left the station, rounded a bend, and, suddenly, all I had ever known of home was gone from sight. I missed you all so much my heart ached.

As the train sped along, the world outside changed quickly, our oaks and sycamores and elms giving way to "scrub oaks" and, finally, and this just on the other side of Fort Worth, the mesquite trees began, and these seem to flourish all through this country. They are quite lovely in a small way, light green and delicately lacy.

The batiste robe and gown you made for my going away presents are exquisite. The stitches in the little tucks are so fine as to be almost invisible, and the embroidered rosebuds look as if they might begin opening momentarily.

Aunt Catherine, take good care of yourself. Nothing more must change. I know Papa's death was a great blow to you, but his children, every one of us, think of you as another mother, and not many are lucky enough to have two.

Love,
Lucy

JANE ROBERTS WOOD

Dearest Lillian,

I have met the man I just might marry. My dear sister, there is so much to tell you I hardly know where to begin.

By the time we left Dallas, in spite of the tears, or perhaps, because of them, I felt wonderful. My navy serge skirt does match the blue of my eyes, and my middy blouse is *très élégante*. Wearing your ostrich hat, I felt like an illustration in the *Delineator*.

In Fort Worth we were delayed almost an hour by the late arrival of the train from the East. There two men boarded the train and took a seat just across the aisle from me. Although they were wearing suits, their boots and broad-brimmed hats suggested a ranching background.

In order to make myself a little more comfortable, I crossed my legs and immediately heard Mama's voice saying, "Lucy, ladies do not cross their limbs in public," so I uncrossed mine and giggled. At once the short, red-faced man across the aisle was up and over. "Howdy," he said. "I'm Jimmy Green." His Irish brogue and wide smile were irresistible to me. "I'm Lucinda Richards," I said, offering my hand.

"Where you headin', Miss Richards?" he asked. When I told him I was going to teach at White Star, he said, "Well if that ain't somethin'! I work the Sully ranch, and your school is *on* the ranch!" Then he gestured over his shoulder toward his traveling companion, a somewhat younger man, and said, "This here's Bob Sully. His old man owns all the Sully ranches." Then, raising his voice, "Hey, Bob, come on over here and meet White Star's new

4

teacher." Taking off his hat, Mr. Sully stood up, and I was looking into the bluest eyes I've ever seen. His hair is the color of your new gold wedding band, and his dark skin attests to his having spent most of his life out-of-doors.

"Miss Richards, let me tell you about the teacher that was run off from White Star last year," Jimmy Green said, chuckling.

But Mr. Sully interrupted him. "Gol-dern it, Jimmy. We don't want Miss Richards to turn right around and go back home. We need a teacher at White Star. Where you from?" When I told him I was from Bonham, he said, "That's blackland cotton country, isn't it? All I know is ranching," and he smiled and blushed so that he might as well have added that he knows nothing about young ladies. His shyness gave me the courage to unpack the lunch basket Aunt Catherine had prepared and ask them to share it with me.

Mr. Green said, "Oh, no, Ma'am. We wouldn't want to eat your lunch," and he picked up a drumstick and took a big bite.

Then Mr. Sully said, "Sometimes that morning stage runs late. You might get awful hungry before you get to White Star," and he took a thigh. By the time I had persuaded them to join me, all the fried chicken was gone and most of the chocolate cake.

My new acquaintances had been to New York to pick up what they called their "wolf hunters." Mr. Green, who did most of the talking, said that last year the Sullys had lost over a thousand sheep to wolves on one of their ranches. He said, "The Old Man made up his mind he was through with *that*, and he sent all the way to Russia for some wolfhounds, then double-jobbed me and Bob to New York to pick 'em up."

Mr. Green entertained me all the way to Wichita Falls by telling stories about how the last three teachers at White Star had been "run off." In Wichita Falls, Mr. Sully, embarrassed but enjoying the conversation, stood and said, "Miss Richards, I'll be here at the Henrietta ranch for two or three days. Then I'll be at the White Star for most of the fall. My mother would enjoy a visit from a young lady, and I . . ."

He looked so helplessly confused that I laughed, but then quickly said, "I would like that very much, Mr. Sully."

"Well then," he said, putting on his hat, "you just send me a note by my brother, Dickie. He'll be one of your students. You let me know when you can come." As the train slowed at Wichita Falls, little more than a shed at a crossing, seven or eight cowboys came galloping up and escorted us to our stop. One was leading a big, black horse, a horse that even I could tell was finer, more spirited than the others. Mr. Green said, "Well gol-dern, Bob. They've brought your horse. Looks like I'll be going home alone on the wagon with the gear."

"The Old Man probably thought I needed to ride along with the hounds," Bob replied and then he turned to me. "That's old Surprise. Ain't he a beaut?" And he was just that. A beaut! When the train stopped, Mr. Sully and Mr. Green jumped off to unload the wolfhounds. In their high-heeled boots, they ran awkwardly alongside the train to the baggage car, and the other cowboys followed on horseback, riding back and forth alongside the tracks, sometimes circling the two as they ran. As the horses were rearing and skittering sideways, terrified of the train, Mr. Sully called out "Come on, boys. Let's unload 'em."

THE TRAIN TO ESTELLINE

I stepped off the train and watched as they slid open the side doors of the baggage car and unloaded a dozen huge wooden crates, each containing a large white Russian wolfhound. By now a small crowd had gathered. Mr. Sully said, "Let 'em out, Jimmy. They'll follow the horses," and he jumped on his horse as Mr. Green opened the first of the cage doors. Then Mr. Sully and the cowboys started back the way they had come, riding at an easy lope across the wide plains and, one by one, the majestic dogs effortlessly caught up with the riders and then led the way, seeming to know instinctively when the men on horseback were going to turn to the right or the left.

Mr. Green, left behind, walked back to where I was standing. "One way or another the Sullys ain't gonna lose no more sheep to them wolves," he said. I offered my hand and told him I hoped to see him soon. "Yes, Ma'am, Miss Richards, at White Star real soon," and he tipped his hat and walked away.

Last night on the train, Lillian, waking only when the conductor called out "Electra," "Chillicothe," "Quanah," "Childress," and, just as the sun rose, "Estelline," I dreamed of that moment, the magnificent aristocratic animals running easily ahead of the motley assortment of men on horseback, motley except for Mr. Sully on his beautiful Surprise. That picture remains in my mind like a poem.

Do write me often. As I sit here in my room at Mrs. Gamp's boarding house waiting for the stage which will take me to White Star, I wonder what the Dawsons are like. If I am to live with them for my first three months, I hope we like each other.

Your loving sister,
Lucy

P. S. Tomorrow you will have been married three months. What is it like? Is it bliss when you and Edmund close the bedroom door?

My sweet sister, you have always been beautiful, but since your marriage you have been radiantly so. Even Mr. Walker said, "That sister of yours! She is a great beauty." How wonderful to be thought a great beauty.

September 1, 1911
White Star

Dearest Katie,

After a short rest in Estelline, I took a local stage, that the Sullys operate for the benefit of their ranch hands, on to White Star. Such an adventure! How I wished for my little sister. To get a better view of West Texas, I rode up on the seat with Shorty, the stage driver, all the way to White Star. Katie, this land looks as if a child might have colored it, first with red then, adding great patches of white and, along the walls of the creek beds, blending into the white, faint streaks of blue. It is quite different from our own rich black land.

From my high seat behind four horses, I saw jack-rabbits and prairie dogs, and at a windmill where we stopped to water the horses, I held a tiny horned toad in the palm of my hand. Until we turned off the old cattle trail, birds that Shorty called "telephone birds" perched along the newly strung wires. One is like the mourning doves we have in our own backyard. Another, called a "scissor-tail," I had not noticed before. It appears a black and silver streak when it chases some insect, invisible to my eye, but as it reaches the top of its flight, it spreads its wings and tail, and then it seems as if a bright flower has blossomed against the sky.

Mr. Giles Dawson was waiting for me when the stagecoach arrived, and by nightfall I will be in the house where I am to spend the next three months. After two days of traveling, I look forward to a good supper, a hot bath, and a soft bed.

Mr. Dawson seems a shy, hardworking farmer. His face and hands are as worn as his unpressed overalls. After he had introduced himself, he said, "I'll be awhile gittin' supplies," and he walked across the street to the White Star Feed and Seed Store.

I stretched my legs by walking through White Star two or three times. Besides the store, where Mr. Dawson is now loading his wagon, there is a post office, a blacksmith shop next to it, a small white Baptist church, a busy cotton gin, and a dozen or more houses clustered around.

As I sat on a bench in front of the seed store, a man standing on a split-log road grader approached driving two spotted mules. The difference between the rutty, bumpy streak of dirt before him and the smooth-shaven path he was leaving set me to wondering what effect my teaching might have in White Star.

Do write me often. I am far away from all I've ever known.

Hugs and kisses,
Lucy

JANE ROBERTS WOOD

September 3, 1911
At the Dawson's

Dear Diary,

During the last miles of my journey, the silence between Mr. Dawson and me was almost a relief. I had never been so tired. My bones ached. When I fastened my cape against the wind, my hands trembled. I longed for sleep.

After about three hours (at a spot that had no discernible markings), we turned off the wagon trail and drove across a bare prairie. The house toward which we were headed was the only one in the landscape and it, this lone house, made the countryside seem more desolate than if there had been no house there at all. As we drew nearer, I saw that a barbed wire fence encircled the house. I wondered what it kept in. Or out. Not the chickens that pecked disconsolately in the bare yard. Nor the cow tied to a mesquite in front.

Mrs. Dawson stood on the porch. Her hair was pulled sharply up into a bun in back. Her dress that could never have been other than drab was covered with a dingy apron. "Hidy," she said. "Come on in." Her hands were busy, rolling themselves up into her apron.

The Dawson's house, when I entered it, made my mouth run dry; the hairs on my arms stood up. I wanted to run, but instead I stumbled up the stairs to the room where I was led and fell across the bed and slept.

I have been here three days now, waiting for the strength to leave. I cannot stay. Mrs. Dawson said the gypsum water made me sick, but Mrs. Dawson's wrong. It was the musty, grit-filled sheets, cold cornbread and blue milk for supper, the raw unpainted walls in my bedroom. And the odor! Overall a smell of sour milk, stale sweat, despair—of something unearthed or uncloseted and *nothing* to suggest tomorrow or Christmas. Most terrible of all is the long tapeworm in a jar on the kitchen table that Mr. Dawson, toothless and unshaven, proudly showed me, a tapeworm that he said was removed from his own body.

At night I lie in bed desperately trying not to hear the howling of the wind, a keening that goes to the bone's marrow. Each time it dies away, I hope that the stillness will last, but it only uses these moments to gather itself for a more penetrating assault. This is a world of anguished sounds.

This morning I drank a cup of tea. Tomorrow I will walk to the schoolhouse. I will look at what was to have been my great adventure. I will take a good, long look at it, and then I will ask Mr. Dawson to drive me in to White Star to catch the stage. I cannot stay here.

I'm going home.

Sadly,
Lucy

September 4, 1911
At the Dawson's

Dear Diary,

I've taken a turn for the better, and the why of it is a mystery to me.

The wind stopped blowing today, and I walked to the schoolhouse. At first I felt unsteady, inside more than out, but after I had walked the mile-and-a-half stretch between the Dawson's and the school, I sat on the steps in the warm sunshine and looked at the sky, whitewashed to a pale blue and gentled by close, slow-moving clouds, all the time thinking I had just come to say goodbye.

Then I walked inside and saw the sun shining through the window, the dust motes light and dancing, and the benches and desks all huddled in one dark corner. In a minute, I had them all in rows and then I dusted them off with a wisp of a broom I found.

Now I've decided to stay, for a month or so. Maybe even as long as Thanksgiving.

Love,
Lucy

P.S. Diary, maybe it *was* the gypsum water that made me sick.

September 5, 1911
At the Dawson's

Dear Mr. Sully,

The school is in deplorable condition, dirty and grim. Books, chalk, and erasers—*all* essentials are in short supply or nonexistent, and Mr. Dawson says the empty woodbox is my responsibility.

Much work is needed if school is to begin in two weeks. The building must be cleaned and whitewashed, inside and out. Then the brush must be cleared from the schoolground and the merry-go-round and swings repaired.

I shall be glad to take care of the cleaning, but for the other tasks I need help. I know you agree that we must do all we can to make learning a pleasant experience for your son Dickie and the other students.

Sincerely,
Lucy Eliza Richards

THE TRAIN TO ESTELLINE

September 7, 1911
At the Dawson's

Dear George,

I am sorry you did not hear Woodrow Wilson at the Dallas State Fair. The hardware store is simply too confining. Have you spoken to Mama about selling it? Does she know how much you dislike selling onion slips and porch swings day after day?

George, wherever you decide to go, do not come out here. This country is more desolate than any place you can imagine. Oklahoma is the place for you to be. With the oil boom, a young man could make a fortune there. Find a way to follow your heart.

Love,
Lucy

September 8, 1911
At the Dawson's

Dearest Lillian,

Oh, my dear sister! Your letter, along with George's, came today telling me you are expecting a sweet baby in the spring. I am so happy. I want the baby to be a girl and to look just like Katie. But, a little auburn-haired, blue-eyed girl just like her mother would be perfect too. Please send some pink yarn, lots of it, so her Aunt Lucy can start right away on a present.

Have you told Mama yet? I know she thinks it unseemly to have a baby the first year of marriage, but when she has adjusted to the idea, she will be as happy as I am.

Sit down while you read the rest of this letter. A tragedy occurred during my stagecoach ride out here, and I have not, until now, had the courage to tell you about it.

Just two hours from White Star, Shorty, the driver, looked across the prairie and said, "Miz. Richards, we're in fer it. Better git inside. Yonder's a blue norther comin'." Lillian, I was so happy about meeting Mr. Sully that I felt the world was too splendid to ride through enclosed in a stagecoach. I refused, saying I wanted to see the country from the best view. I survived the blue norther, but your hat did not. After the knife-chilling wind had died away, Shorty glanced toward me and began to laugh. Not one feather was left on your beautiful hat, and I must have looked like a plucked chicken. With what dignity I could muster, I took off the hat and sailed it out into the brush, not wishing my hosts to be as amused as Shorty.

I need not have worried! Nothing amuses the Dawsons. No smile, no teasing remark, no surprise on the kitchen table—nothing brings an answering smile or a pleasant remark to their lips.

There is no beauty here. Although the Dawsons own this small farm, nothing comes into fullness on it. No flowers bloom; no color brightens the house; no smell of soup cooking warms the heart. My bedroom has neither wallpaper nor paint. At night I spread my bright red cape across the foot of the bed, both for warmth and color, and I keep the drab curtains, strung across a corner of the room for a closet, drawn back so my clothes can brighten the room.

Yesterday, Mr. Bob Sully brightened my day with a present! I was cleaning the schoolroom when he rode up on his beautiful horse, unbuttoned his shirt and took from it the most adorable five-week old puppy I have ever seen, a small bundle of sniffs and tail-waggings and pink-tongued licks. He said, "I hope they make good pets. Try him and see." And with that he got down off his horse and, while I played with the little wolfhound puppy, he drew a tub of water from the well for cleaning. That afternoon his father sent over two ranch hands, and together they whitewashed the school, chopped wood until the woodbox was filled and overflowing, and then cut the brush from the schoolground. We even swept the schoolhouse yard clean of burrs and nettles. Can you imagine sweeping a yard? Much remains to be done, but the walls are sparkling white, the floors are clean, and I will be ready to welcome my dozen or so students in a week.

Mr. Sully said he would stop by again soon. Even now I look out my bedroom window, hoping to see that straight, slender figure riding across the prairie to my door.

Love,
Lucy

September 10, 1911
At the Dawson's

Dear Mama,

I hope you have not been too worried about me. I am feeling better, cheered by a freshly cleaned schoolroom and by my little puppy that I've named "His Highness" because of his proud bearing. This I've shortened to "H.H.," and already he knows his name.

I cannot imagine why the Dawsons agreed to offer me room and board for a month. They have no children in school, and Mr. Dawson is not a school trustee. Although they are furnishing my keep, I am paying them to feed

H.H. When Mr. Dawson saw him, he said, "Costs to feed dogs," and I said, "Mr. Dawson, I will, of course, pay for H.H.'s keep."

I know I've lost weight since I have been here. Each morning Mrs. Dawson sends me off to the schoolhouse with a syrup bucket into which she has poured red beans topped with a piece of cornbread and a slice of onion. I long for the cucumber and chicken salad sandwiches you used to make for my school lunches. Oh, and Aunt Catherine's hot tea cookies! H.H., however, is not so discriminating. He wolfs down every bite.

Yesterday, I went in to White Star with Mr. Dawson to get supplies, and I found an excellent milliner there, a Miss Elam. I ordered a lavender hat covered with flowers in shades of pink and lavender. Spring is months away, but having such a lovely hat hanging on my wall will take some of the drabness from my room.

Although I still plan to resign by Thanksgiving, I am excited about the first day of school. Today, from the dry creek bed, I gathered silver, green, and golden grasses and put them in the schoolroom and by my bed. Mr. Dawson did not comment on the lovely look and smell of the pitcher of sage I placed on the kitchen table, but when he came in from milking, he stood gazing at it for a long minute.

Mama, please make a bonnet and send it to me. The wind blows every day, and my face is getting quite brown. I do not want to look like a field hand.

Love,
Lucy

THE TRAIN TO ESTELLINE

September 17, 1911
At the Dawson's

Dearest Aunt Catherine,

On the first day of school eleven students had arrived by eight-thirty. By the time the day was over, George Sams' horse had strayed and he had to be excused from arithmetic to find him; "Little 'Un" Sams had cried for his mother all morning; Jinks Mayfield had gone home, just walked off, because the Baldridge twins announced they couldn't play with her because she had the "itch," and Bucy Abernathy, one year older than I, leaned back in his seat all morning as if to say, "Teach me if you can!"

Oh, how I tried. I rushed from one to the other, giving each an assignment, and trying to return to check the work by the time it was completed.

Most of them tried. Only Bucy refused to attempt his assignment. He was not openly defiant, and I did not force a confrontation. I do not want to be the fourth teacher "run-off" from White Star, but Bucy must try if he stays in my schoolroom.

Aunt Catherine, I am so happy you are making a wedding ring quilt for my hope chest. It will be such a treasure, always.

Love,
Lucy

September 19, 1911
At the Dawson's

Dear Mr. Sully,

If I am to teach the children in the community, please advise the school board that the following supplies are needed immediately:

1 box of chalk
6 erasers
1 Dictionary
3 McGuffy's Primers
5 McGuffey's Eclectic Readers
8 Webster's Blue Back Spellers
8 Ray's Eclectic Arithmetic books
Please furnish these as soon as possible.

Sincerely,
Lucy Eliza Richards

September 24, 1911
At the Dawson's

Dear Mr. and Mrs. Sully,

Your son, Dickie, has been bringing his pistol, which he says is needed for protection from rattlesnakes, to school. In the future, he simply will have to avoid any snakes which happen to be in his path. He disrupted the reading lesson today when he shot a rabbit through the schoolroom window. Until the sudden and alarming noise, I was unaware that the gun was real. This rule also includes knives.

I have written notes to the parents of all the students informing them of this rule.

Sincerely,
Lucy Eliza Richards

September 27, 1911
At the Dawson's

Dear Mrs. Sully,

Dickie brought your kind note, inviting me to spend the weekend of October 5 with you at the ranch. I shall be happy to come, and I look forward to meeting you and Mr. Sully with great pleasure. I agree that we have much to discuss.

Lucy Richards

September 29, 1911
At the Dawson's

Dear Mr. Sully,

I hope the trustees have not already purchased the supplies which I requested. Until yesterday, I did not know Mr. Constable's two children would not begin the school year until all the cotton was in. Please amend the book order to:

4 McGuffy's Primers
6 McGuffey's Eclectic Readers
10 Webster's Blue Back Spellers
10 Ray's Eclectic Arithmetic books

Sincerely,
Lucy Eliza Richards

October 1, 1911
At the Dawson's

Dearest Aunt Catherine,

How I needed your nursing skills this past Friday. It was a crisp and clear September day, so perfect I had allowed my students an extra fifteen minutes for lunch. However, when I rang the school bell, the oldest of them, Squint Constable, did not appear. Neither did H.H. Dickie Sully, an adorable, smaller version of his older brother, said he had last seen Squint walking toward the Red River with H.H. following closely behind. Thinking of the treacherous quicksand in the river bed, I was suddenly quite frightened for my little puppy. The children and I went to look for them, and we had not walked five minutes when we heard H.H.'s shrill barking. We found him barking frantically into the mouth of an abandoned well.

Keeping the others well back, Petey Constable and I carefully leaned over the well's edge. "Hey, it's Squint down there," Petey said. "Hang on a minute, Squint, and I'll throw you a rope."

"Won't do no good," Squint answered. "Leg's broke."

Trying to be very calm, I sent Big 'Un Sams to the Dawson's and Bucy to the Constable farm for help.

I kept the younger children well back and called down frequent encouragement to Squint. Little Dickie Sully and Petey, afraid I would fall in, hung on tightly to my skirt. In no time Big 'Un was back with the news that the Dawsons were not at home. I looked at Big 'Un's six-foot frame and knew he was far too heavy for me to lower into the well. Oh, Aunt Catherine, to think of going down into that horrible black hole with who knows what crawling creatures at its bottom! Only the piteous sound of Squint's moans caused me to put my foot in a loop that Big 'Un quickly made, hold on tightly, and allow myself to be lowered. Squint was quite nauseated, and I held his head in my arms. Petey found two more or less straight sticks, and I tore up my petticoat for a splint, but I felt unable to set the leg. However, I offered some comfort, bathing Squint's face from a bucket of water that Petey lowered. When Squint said, "I appreciate it, Ma'am," I was glad I had found the courage to be there.

After a while, I heard the sounds of an automobile and then a deep voice. I knew help had arrived, and there was never a more welcome sound to my ears.

Tomorrow, I plan to begin a medicine chest like the one you keep at the foot of your bed. When I was a little girl, what a comfort it was to see you open the lid of that trunk, knowing as I did that it contained medicine and supplies to lessen any pain, lower any fever, repair any bone.

How is my beautiful quilt progressing? Since Lillian is confined to her bed, couldn't she piece a few squares to hurry it along?

Love,
Lucy

October 2, 1911
At the Dawson's

Dear Mrs. Sully,

One of my students, Squint Constable, fell in the well and suffered a broken leg. Because he is recovering at the schoolhouse, I will not be able to come to the ranch this weekend. May I postpone my visit for a week?

H.H., the adorable puppy your son gave me, has won everyone's heart. Had it not been for his frantic barking, we might not have discovered Squint at all.

Sincerely,
Lucy Eliza Richards

October 4, 1911
At the Dawson's

Dear Lillian,

H.H. and I, in a small way, are heroes in the community, and I have met Josh Morris Arnold, the school principal in Estelline. Lillian, there is no way to describe this man. His voice booms over the Texas prairie, and he is a whirlwind of energy. He has the most beautiful Tennessee accent I have ever heard. His hair is black as a blackbird's wing, and his eyes are as green as an East Texas spring meadow.

He was on his way to spend the weekend at the Constable farm, and so it was he who answered my distress call when Squint had to be rescued from the well. He quickly pulled me out, lowered himself into the well, splinted Squint's leg and devised a sling with which to pull him out. He made this seem effortless as all the while he consoled, cajoled, and reassured the injured boy.

Because Squint was nauseated and in pain, his family decided not to move him. We made the patient comfortable in the schoolhouse on a cot lent grudgingly by the Dawsons. Mr. Constable made his son drink one-half of a bottle of Universal Liver Remedy, and then Squint's family returned to their farm and its chores. Mrs. Constable will come tomorrow to decide if the leg is broken or just badly sprained. Her husband believes that she's a natural healer, a kind of West Texas witch doctor.

After the Constables left, Mr. Arnold made a fire to take the chill off the room, and when Squint had dozed off, he brought me a dipper of sweet water. When I mentioned that there had been a surprising number of bottles, unbroken ones, in the bottom of the old well, he threw back his head and laughed. "So, that's what

Squint was doing in the well. Hiding tequila." Before I could absorb the meaning of this remark, he had disappeared in the direction of the well. When he returned with a bottle in his hand, I knew he had gone down into the well to retrieve some of the liquor.

Without asking permission, he took a drink from the bottle. Then we sat and talked as the sun fell below the horizon, and a single star came out and hung there. Mr. Arnold told me how precious water is to the West Texans, and of how their longing, their love for it is reflected in their daily conversation and in their religion. He said, "Go to a brush arbor revival some Sunday and listen to the reverence with which they sing, 'Shall We Gather At The River' or 'Roll Jordan Roll.' It's not heaven for which they long; it's pure fresh sweet water, like the water in that dipper you hold in your hands."

I was struck with the idea of a brush arbor revival. I wondered what that might be. As he talked, the rest of the stars, thousands of them, appeared, filling the sky. Josh stood and began to walk back and forth. "One day water will be brought to this country," he said, "from the ocean or up from the ground. Then this dry desert will become a fertile plain. Oh, this country has a great future, and I intend to be a part of it."

Mama wrote me that you had been confined to your bed for two long weeks. I hope and pray you feel more comfortable now. Of course, I do not mind if the baby is a boy. He might grow to be as handsome as his father or just like little Dickie Sully, who has quite won my heart. Both the Sullys have sweet, gentle natures, enhanced by innate good manners. I look forward to meeting the rest of them.

If you feel well enough, please help Aunt Catherine

with my quilt. Next weekend will be my first chance to spend long hours in Mr. Sully's company, but I know our friendship will grow into something much stronger.

Love,
Lucy

October 5, 1911
At the Dawson's

Dear Diary,

Last Friday Mr. Arnold poured a little tequila into a cup of water and said, "Miss Richards, compare this to your Bonham wine." So I drank that cupful and then another.

The moon was high when he drove away and I tiptoed up to bed. There it was again, the moon, now just outside my window, washed to a pale silver by the soft glow of the stars shining all around. As I took off my clothes, the wind quickened, a little freshet, and the moon swayed and I was dancing, cradling my breasts in my arms, moving in time to the silent sound of the wind that I knew was waiting, gathering itself to come surging across the canyons and fields, up over the Caprock, and across the prairie. Finally, I fell into bed and dreamed all night, strange sweet dreams I cannot now remember.

When I woke up, it was mid-morning, and Mrs. Dawson was calling up the stairs, asking if I was all right, and saying Mrs. Constable had come at sunrise to take Squint home. I walked to the schoolhouse and found a spice cake that Mrs. Constable had left for me. Just a plain, dark brown cake there on my desk but filling the room with the smell of sun tea and cloves.

Back in the kitchen, Mrs. Dawson politely moved the

tapeworm jar from the table, Mr. Dawson already out mending a chicken coop, and together we had morning coffee and cake. "That woman," she said, carefully sorting through and choosing each word, "that Mrs. Constable. Hands as soft and white as a girl's. As yours." And she looked down at hers, bruised and reddened, lying helplessly in her lap, like two small, wounded rabbits.

I will make some yellow curtains for her kitchen window when I leave. I will not drink tequila again. Not with Josh Arnold. Not with anybody.

Love,
Lucy

October 6, 1911
At the Dawson's

Dearest Mama,

Your letter just arrived saying George has left home, bound for Oklahoma. Mama, I am responsible. I urged him to go, and now, if something should happen to him, I could never forgive myself. Please let me know as soon as you hear from him, and if he should write me, I will let you know immediately.

Mama, have you thought of running the hardware business yourself? Papa used to say that you have a better head for business than most men.

Never mind what Bonham would say. It is a new day for women.

Love,
Lucy

October 8, 1911
At the Dawson's

Dear Mr. Arnold,

I am unable to accept your kind invitation to attend a brush arbor meeting with you this Sunday. I have accepted a previously extended invitation, and I plan to attend the Baptist Church in White Star.

Sincerely,
Lucy Richards

October 10, 1911
At the Dawson's

Dear Aunt Catherine,

If I can win the hearts of my students, I believe I can win their minds as well. Since I went down into the well to help Squint (who as it turned out had only a bad sprain), he has been the most obliging of my older students. He comes to class limping but prepared, voices his opinions freely during discussions, and willingly helps the younger students with their sums and reading. Only Bucy Abernathy, clearly the leader of the older students, remains unwilling to cooperate, and I have avoided a confrontation with him until yesterday. Then one was forced upon me.

We had returned from the lunch hour, and I was reading, as is my custom, *Moby Dick*. I felt an unbearable tension in the room, so unlike the usually relaxed, almost sleepy, atmosphere that I could not concentrate on the words I was reading. When I looked up, from time to time, every eye was on me, every back ramrod straight, every pair of hands clenched tightly on the desk tops.

I took a deep breath, laid my book down, and said, "What is it?" No one spoke or moved. I realized the students were stealing quick glances toward Bucy Abernathy. I asked, "Bucy, what is it?" His only response was an indifferent shrug of his shoulders. Then he gazed out the window as if none of this concerned him. I then turned my gaze on Dickie Sully. His eyes widened, his face turned red, and the words, "Bucy Abernathy spit in the well. Three times!" exploded from his mouth.

Squint's shocked astonishment made me realize the seriousness of the act.

"Bucy, is this true?"

Another shrug.

"Bucy, step outside, please." As I continued reading, I was all too aware of Bucy's slow, careless saunter as he left the room, and I prayed the chapter would never end. I had no idea what I would say when I confronted him. Physical punishment seemed out of the question for a boy older than I and a head taller, but I knew that the next fifteen minutes might well determine my future at the school.

Spitting in the well. In Bonham, the water is stored in tanks, but here the wells are often uncovered, and the water is so precious as to be almost sacred.

I finished the chapter, gave each student an assignment, and walked outside, hoping Bucy would have disappeared or, perhaps, jumped into the well he had so desecrated.

He stood just outside the door, with his back toward me, his arms crossed. A great tall boy.

"Bucy?" I was so frightened I could only whisper the name.

He turned toward me, his face flushed. "Aw, Miz. Richards," he said. And he could say no more. Bucy Abernathy was crying!

"Why, Bucy." I was more astonished than if *I* had spat in the well.

"I can't read," he said. "I hate this school. Dickie Sully can read bettern' me, and he's eight. I've tried to find the words everybody else sees, but I just can't find the dern things."

Oh, the relief I felt!

"Bucy Abernathy, I can teach anybody to read, but I can't cut wood. When we need more wood, you cut it. And, I'll stay after school for thirty minutes every day, and I'll teach you to read."

Aunt Catherine, if you were here you could teach him. I remember how you taught me my times tables. Cookies and hugs are great motivators.

Love,
Lucy

P.S. Here is a scrap from Dickie Sully's shirt. He tore this great patch out when he suddenly jumped through the schoolroom window to pounce, like a cat, on a baby quail. I'd like it in my quilt.

October 11, 1911
At the Dawson's

Dear Mr. Arnold,

Bucy Abernathy and I work together every day on his reading. He knows math, but words remain a mystery to him.

If you have any new methods, please share them with me.

Sincerely,
L. E. Richards

October 12, 1911
The Sully Ranch

Dearest Maggie,

I'm glad Mama gave you my address when you stopped at the hardware store last week. George has always thought you were one of the prettiest girls in Bonham, and he would appreciate a letter from you. When I hear from him, I will certainly send him your address.

When we graduated from high school, you wrote in my autograph book:

When you get married
And live on a hill,
Send me a kiss
By the whippoorwill.

Neither the whippoorwill nor the hill seem a part of my immediate future, but I have met an attractive young man, Bob Sully, and I am spending the weekend on the Sully ranch.

I write this letter sitting in a guest bedroom with white starched curtains, pink rose-sprigged wallpaper, and an imported pink marble fireplace in which a small fire cheerfully burns to take the chill from the room. When it warms up a little, Mr. Sully and I plan to ride out to a line camp, whatever that is. I hope I can manage to stay on the horse.

Maggie, working in your father's bank must be reassuring as well as challenging. When we were in the fifth grade, I walked by the bank on Easter Sunday, and there you were in the window all dressed up in your Easter finery. Your daddy was sitting at his desk basking in the admiration from all the people who walked by enjoying you in your new dress. I suppose that was as much of an Easter Parade as Bonham ever had.

My adorable little Dickie Sully just knocked on my door bringing me an early blooming Christmas cactus. He had dug it up and potted it for me. Now he has taken H.H. for a walk around the ranch. He is always busy. I never knew how fervently little boys could love their teachers. He watches me all the time, but when I look at him, he blushes—much like his older brother. However, I do *not* think his father should allow him to carry a gun around the ranch.

Please write again soon. Old chums (I'll be eighteen in one month) must keep in touch with each other.

Your best chum,
Lucy

October 12, 1911
The Sully Ranch

Dearest Diary,

The great adventure has begun. I am thrilled I decided to stay. Writing Maggie Owens, "lording it over her," as Aunt Catherine would say, is delicious, and now all that's lacking is Bob's proposal.

But I'm not so sure Mrs. Sully wants her older son to marry me, although last night she couldn't have been sweeter. She asked politely about my family, being careful not to pry. She said she knew my mother must miss me, and she wondered if my father and mother would be coming out to see me. When I told her Papa had died so recently, she hugged me and kissed my cheek, seeming genuinely grieved. Then she said she'd never been to the Dawson's and asked if I am comfortable there. Some distance between us kept me from telling her how uncomfortable I am, and I answered that I have become accustomed to the household.

But during family prayers, a Sully custom every night, I glanced her way when she prayed for Papa's soul and was startled to meet her pale, blue eyes, wide-open and staring into mine.

Unsettled,
Lucy

October 13, 1911
The Sully Ranch

Dearest Mama,

A terrible thing has happened to Dickie Sully. Young Mr. Sully and I were just this evening returning from a visit to a line camp when we heard three shots fired in rapid succession. We stopped our horses, listened, and heard three more shots. Mr. Sully grabbed the reins of my horse and said, "Something's happened at the house. Hang on!" With that he spurred Surprise, I clung to my saddle horn, and we galloped the horses all the way home.

When we arrived, one of the Mexicans took the horses and we ran into the house. Miss Grace Sully, his aunt, grabbed his arm and took him into the library. When he came out, he told me Dickie (even as I write this, I cannot believe it), had fallen from a windmill and was now lying unconscious on his mother's bed. One by one we tiptoed in, knelt by the bed, and for a few minutes joined his mother in prayer.

As soon as Dickie was brought from the pasture, lying on a barn door his father had shot away from its hinges, his mother took her position there by his bed and has not left it.

Mr. Sully went to the telephone immediately (thank goodness they had just installed one), and called both a doctor from Childress and one from Amarillo to come. If he can just live until tomorrow, I know these doctors can make him well again.

Your worried,
Lucy

October 14, 1911
At the Sully Ranch

Dearest Aunt Catherine,

Since I wrote Mama, nothing has changed. Dickie has not regained consciousness. His mother remains by his bedside, praying. His father paces up and down the walk in front of the house as if his urgency can somehow speed the doctors on their way.

This morning Dickie's head is slightly swollen and his bruises more pronounced. His hands, begrimed and scratched from play, lie still, folded quietly over the covers, and this, the stillness of his hands, is astonishingly sad. I do not believe I will be able to go back into that room again.

The whole house is quiet, but the sun has just come up and with it our hopes. Miss Grace Sully, returning from the sickroom, says Dickie's face now has a little more color.

Bob is withdrawn and looks my way only occasionally as if to say, "Who are you? What are you doing here?" I can understand his worry with all my heart.

His father, on the other hand, seems to be glad for my presence. On the front porch just now he said, "So, Miss Richards, no guns or knives in your school—eh? Well, quite right! But, you are the first teacher we have ever had to take any notice of it." And he added, "Well, Dickie will be back in school soon. The boy thinks a lot of you." Then he looked bewildered, as if suddenly realizing that the once bright mind might be irreparably damaged.

I wish I could have your arms around me for just one minute.

Love,
Lucy

October 14, 1911
At the Sully Ranch

Dearest Lillian,

Because everything possible is being done for Dickie, my thoughts, just this morning, turn anxiously toward Bob Sully and his strange behavior. He had been so tender and sweet during our ride out to the line camp. When we stopped to rest our horses, he had placed his hands on my shoulders and, turning me around in a circle, he said, "Look, Lucy. Look at this land. I want you to love this country the way I do."

But since the accident, Bob has looked at me without seeing me, heard my voice without responding. I would assume that he is simply in shock, but his eyes and ears are finely tuned to his mother's every sign, every prayer, every gesture. She wondered aloud how Dickie, as sure-footed as a mountain goat, could have fallen, and Bob rode immediately to the site of the accident. She said she wanted Dickie to have his favorite fruit, peaches, when he recovered, and Bob went into White Star to find some.

Oh, even as I write this I feel small and selfish. Please forgive this pettiness and know these feelings spring from fatigue and grief rather than jealousy.

The strain is beginning to tell on us all. While I sat with Miss Grace Sully just outside Dickie's bedroom just now, Mr. Sully walked past, opened the bedroom door, and motioned his wife to come outside.

"Mrs. Sully, I want you to consider asking Mrs. Constable to come look at Dickie. At least, consider . . ."

"I'll not have it!" she said sharply. "Mr. Sully, if that woman comes into Dickie's room, she comes over my dead body."

At this his sister spoke up. "Robert Sully, have you gone crazy? The finest doctors in West Texas on their way out here and you asking Dickie's mother to let some mumbo jumbo woman touch him! Certainly not!"

Mr. Sully stood for a minute, and then he turned and walked away. Although I agree with them, I grieve for this desperate father, grasping at straws.

Love,
Lucy

October 14, 1911
At the Sully Ranch

Dearest Mama,

The doctors, each one accompanied by a nurse, arrived today, one at ten this morning and another at two. After an examination and a consultation with Mr. and

Mrs. Sully, Dickie was tenderly placed on the dining room table where he was operated upon to relieve the pressure caused by his head injury. After the surgery, Dr. Otis Stone told the family that medicine could do nothing more. Now we can only wait and hope and pray.

I look at Mrs. Sully and wonder what thoughts go on behind her pale blue eyes. She appears, for the most part, serene and composed. Her religion offers much consolation, but she must also be comforted by the vast sums of money that lie at her disposal, money which provides the finest care and the most advanced knowledge for her poor wounded child. What a difference between Squint Constable's accident and the Sully tragedy! Here, the world has stopped; this is in itself a luxury. The Sullys wait silently and patiently for it to begin turning again on its axis, that axis being one small, much-loved boy. Had Squint been seriously injured when he fell into the well, his family, without any hired help, would have had to go right on with the milking and feeding and fence mending. How much better to be rich when misfortune comes!

Jimmy Green is driving me to the Dawson's this evening. Although the Sully ranch house has seventeen rooms, these are barely adequate to meet the extra demands placed on the house by the medical staff. And I must prepare my Monday classes.

I received no letters from home this week, but I know the hardware store keeps you busy.

Love,
Lucy

October 15, 1911
At the Dawson's

Dearest Mama,

Bob Sully rode over to tell me that Dickie Sully died at 4:00 this morning. Such a bright and cheerful little boy. The force of his presence was out of all proportion to his size.

It was a day of anguish, not only for me, but for all my students. We could not bear to look at his empty desk, nor could we seem to look away from it. I emptied his treasures—marbles, a slingshot, a ball of twine, a quail feather, into a sack, and we pushed the desk to a corner of the room. During recess the children spontaneously gathered grasses and berries, anything beautiful, and in glass jars and syrup buckets, arranged their offering on his desk. When H.H. and I returned from a solitary walk, the desk, alive with nature's fall splendor, suggested the funeral barges of the ancient Etruscans, and the loss of one of their princes could not have caused more grief than Dickie's tragic death.

The thought of you at home, happy and busy and well, has been my greatest comfort these past few days.

Love,
Lucy

October 16, 1911
At the Dawson's

Dearest Lillian,

The whole world seems a sad, lost place to me now. I grieve for Dickie Sully, and now my heart goes out to you, my sweet sister. To plan, to wait, to hope for your

covering from his sprained leg, not one meal did Mrs. Dawson send down, not one visit to the schoolroom did she make.

In December I'll be staying at the Constables. Judging from the lunches their children bring to school, the food will be bountiful there. I hope their natures will be too.

I have finished some yellow curtains for the Dawsons. The day I leave I will hang them in their kitchen as a going-away present. Perhaps, then, some other beauty might blossom in this sterile, gray place.

Love,
Lucy

October 25, 1911
At the Dawson's

Dear Mr. Arnold,

I have asked Bucy Abernathy to hand deliver this note. Please come immediately. I need your help!

Gratefully,
Lucy E. Richards

October 26, 1911
At the Dawson's

Dear Lillian,

Yesterday afternoon the children were engaged in a spelling bee when we heard the sound of a horse's hooves. Thinking it must surely be Bob Sully, I was much surprised to see, instead, a strange man riding toward the schoolhouse. A small, dark man, no more than a boy really, walked by his side. As they came nearer, I saw that the boy's hands were tied together with a rope which was then tied to the saddle horn.

I went outside and, knowing a West Texan never dismounts without an invitation, said, "Won't you get off your horse?"

"Well, thanks, Miss Richards," the man said.

"I did not know we had met before," I replied.

"We haven't," he said, "but news of a pretty school teacher travels faster'n a nest of plowed-up jackrabbits." And then he added, "I'm Sheriff Jim Ponder from Childress."

Lillian, how civil these brutal men can be! Sheriff Ponder, riding along Red River, had found this young man, certainly not more than fourteen years of age, wearing a pair of Hamilton Brown boots which Sheriff Ponder said had been stolen from the Sully ranch store. But to Mr. Ponder the most damaging evidence was that the boy was also carrying a length of telegraph wire. Mr. Ponder said, "Why in two shakes of a calf's tail, that wire could be twisted into a branding iron so that Sully calves could be branded and driven across the river into Oklahoma."

Sheriff Ponder lowered the prisoner into the same abandoned well into which Squint had so recently fallen and said, "Miss Richards, I'll drop him off, and, if you don't mind, just feed and water him a time or two. Likely as not, I'll get back by here in a day or so to pick him up and take him into town." Then he laughed and said, "I might just find the time for a visit with you!"

After dinner that evening, I took a pail of food to the well and lowered first the unappetizing fare of beans and cornbread and then a pail of water to the young man. The sun had just fallen below the horizon, and the western sky seemed on fire. I was unable to see clearly into that black, fifteen-foot hole, but I could hear. Oh, how pitiful his cries sounded, echoing up from darkness and helplessness.

Lillian, I want to explain to you, if I can, why I then did what I did. Out here this prairie provides boundless space, so that every emotion —sorrow, joy, anger—expands as if to fill the enormous emptiness. And that boy's sorrow seemed to fill and overflow the well. It swept into my room that night on the bright light of the moon, a light as bright as that of first morning. Finally, I put on my robe, tiptoed down the stairs, and out the door and made my way to the well. With H.H. wagging his tail in encouragement, I tied the rope around my waist, threw one end of it down, and braced myself while the young man climbed out.

"*Gracias, Senora. Gracias, mil gracias,*" he said over and over again.

I said, "*Vamos, vamos!*" knowing that this word in some way means "Now, go away!"

Then I turned and went back into the house and climbed the stairs to my room where I slept the rest of the night, secure in the knowledge that only H.H. and I would ever know just how the boy had managed to climb out of the well.

At breakfast, Mr. Dawson asked, "You fed the Mexican this morning?"

Mrs. Dawson said, "It's too bad to bring him here and dump him. Ain't much use feedin' a thief!"

Then I knew I had made the right choice. I went to the schoolhouse with such a light heart, I skipped all the way. But when I opened the door there he was! There Carlos (for this is his name) was, smiling and nodding and saying, "*Gracias, Senora. Gracias.*"

He seems not to understand my gestures telling him he must leave. He only smiles and shrugs in reply to my urgent *"Vamos! Vamos!"*

I have asked Mr. Arnold to come immediately. For reasons too obvious to mention, I cannot involve Bob Sully in this crisis.

Love,
Lucy

P.S. Mama tells me you have recovered enough to move back to your own house to be with your dear Edmund. When you are completely well again, do come out here. I have much to show you, more to tell you!

October 28, 1911
At the Dawson's

Dear Diary,

In answer to my note, Mr. Arnold motored over on Saturday morning, and before he was out of his automobile he called out, "Miss Richards, are we going to have another tequila party?"

Then I knew it had been a mistake to ask his help. When I told him about Carlos, he threw his head back and laughed that great, rolling laugh of his, a sound that the wind catches up and carries away, bouncing it off across the pasture as it does the giant tumbleweeds.

"I just passed the sheriff," he said when he had stopped laughing. "He must be riding this way now to claim his prisoner. Where is the prisoner, Miss Richards? Is he in the well or out of it?"

Then I felt the fun of it, and laughed too, all the while hearing Mama's voice saying, "Watch out now, Lucinda. Don't throw your bonnet over *his* windmill."

"He's down by the river, gathering firewood," I said, still not sure why I was laughing.

"We've got about five minutes to think of a way to get that Childress sheriff to see things your way," he said.

We sat on the school steps and watched (Lordy, you can see tomorrow out here) as the small, dark speck moving slowly toward us became a beetle, a Centaur and then Sheriff Ponder on his horse.

When he rode into the yard, Josh Arnold was shaking his hand before he'd dismounted, slapping his back, and (a bottle appearing in his hand as if by magic), asking if I wanted a drink, his "Miss Richards?" startling me and the sheriff, then offering a drink to Mr. Ponder as I shook my head.

"So you've come for your prisoner, Jim Ponder? Could you wait a few minutes on that? Miss Richards has that boy gathering firewood down by the river."

At this Sheriff Ponder jerked upright, exclaiming "What in thunder!" but Mr. Arnold went right on as if he hadn't noticed. "It's all she can do to keep the woodbox filled. Miss Richards has just been telling me she spends her Saturdays seeing about the woodbox, cleaning the schoolhouse, dusting the erasers, washing the chalkboard, sweeping the yard. Right now, she should be preparing her lessons, marking papers. But only a few people, Jim, know the value of a really good teacher."

I felt as if I had just listed my Saturday chores and wondered what *he* did on that day. Reading my mind he said, "Now in Estelline . . . , Jim, another drink? It's more of a town than White Star. There people appreciate a teacher. The parents take turns coming in and cleaning. Doing chores."

Mr. Ponder, nodding, took a drink, wiped the mouth of

the bottle with his hand, and passed it back to Mr. Arnold. "Josh," he said, "I got a nephew in your math class. Name's Chester. Chester Davis."

Apparently, Chester Davis is a fine student. Mr. Arnold said he had a good mind and that he knew how to work. Mr. Ponder said he didn't know about that, but he'd sure been getting his math lessons since Josh had whipped him for coming to class without his problems.

Then Josh admired the sheriff's horse, showed him his new motor car (Josh and the Sullys have the only two in the county), and pretty soon the sheriff was leaving, saying he was glad he had brought out a Mexican who could be of help, and tipping his hat, "Miss Richards, you just keep him *at* it. You can have those Saturdays for your teaching."

Josh, looking solemn now, watched him ride away. Then, talking more to himself than to me, he said, "Jim feels good about it. You need the help. But who knows about the boy? Who of us asked him?"

And he turned to me, still unsmiling, "Miss Richards, you've got some help now, and I've got some tequila." I refused, saying I had much to do before Monday's classes. But when he drove away, I felt like a little girl, reprimanded, and not knowing why.

I do not understand Mr. Arnold. I don't want to. With Bob Sully, there's none of this other. There's just Bob and me. It's simple. And nice.

Love,
Lucy

46

October 29, 1911
At the Dawson's

Dear Mr. and Mrs. Sully,

The dozen poplar trees that you sent over are lovingly watered each day by a bucket brigade at our morning recess. You were quite right to send over trees that have root systems which will quickly make their way to the water table below. But until these are established, rest assured that the children and I will provide the water the young trees need.

And, we feel blessed, indeed, knowing that soon we will have, not just a shady spot, but a shade-filled grove for the students to enjoy in the years ahead. This will be a fitting memorial to one who loved the world of nature above all else.

Lucy E. Richards

October 30, 1911
At the Dawson's

Dear Mr. Sully,

I am sorry that you have resigned your position as a trustee of the White Star School. Although you no longer have a child in my classroom (how tragic these words are even as I write them), I know that you value a good education for all the young people in the county. Your response to all our needs has been immediate and effective.

May I make a last request before your resignation becomes effective? I have found a young Mexican, Carlos, who for the past week has assisted with the daily and weekend chores at the school. If the trustees should vote a small stipend for him, that is, enough to pay for his board, I could continue to use this extra time to prepare lessons and mark papers. I am not asking that you furnish a room for Carlos. He sleeps in the schoolhouse and seems quite comfortable there.

Sincerely,
Lucy Eliza Richards

November 3, 1911
At the Dawson's

Dear Diary,

Oh, it's a strange place I've come to. In Bonham, there's a rich bounty of natural beauty—roses and honeysuckle, cedars and oaks, elms, too, and still lakes and pretty little streams and everywhere the greens and yellows.

But here there are only moments of beauty, moments that blossom and hurt the heart, too soon gone. Sunsets, dazzling and bounteous as a benediction. Flights of geese with their symphonies of soft callings and vibrations of wings steadily beating, sounding surprisingly close in this clear, unimpeded air. Or a cactus flower, suddenly at my feet, its droplets of yellow almost hidden by prairie grass.

And the people. Almost always drab and lifeless, but they too can dazzle.

This morning I left Carlos with his Saturday chores at the school, and I washed sheets and clothes, hung them out to dry and then, knowing Mr. Dawson would be in the field grubbing until noon, I asked for use of the kitchen. There, in the blue rinse water left over from the washing, I bathed and washed my hair.

When I'd finished, Mrs. Dawson said she believed she'd just wash her hair too, though it seemed late in the season for such. When she'd finished, and the kitchen was again opened up, I saw how pretty her hair was, drying down around her shoulders. "Mrs. Dawson," I said, "let me do your hair like my sister Lillian's, up at the sides and hanging loose and curled down the back."

"Why, Lucinda, I'm thirty-five," she said. "Too old for that!"

But I got out my rag rollers, and after the dinner dishes were cleared away and Mr. Dawson again in the field, I put her hair up. Just before supper time I brushed it, pulling it up and back at the sides with honey-colored combs, and letting the rest fall almost to her waist in soft cascades of curls. She sat still, hardly breathing, and pleased.

"Now stay there. Just a minute more. Don't move," I said, and I ran upstairs for my lavender hat and white silk shawl.

"Now go look at yourself in the mirror," I said when I'd put the shawl around her shoulders and the hat forward, the shadow of its brim darkening her already dark eyes. At that moment Giles Dawson came from the fields, so it was not his wife that he saw but her mirrored reflection, diffused by the soft glow of the twilight sky and the light from the oil lamp, freshly lit. He said nothing, and I too was mute as the three of us stood there gazing at the quiet, still beauty of the woman in the mirror. Then the hat was gone, the shawl too, both thrust into my hands, and as I turned away, she was putting up her hair, and her husband was going into the kitchen to wash up.

So today nothing is changed after all, and I feel a new sadness by it.

Lucy

JANE ROBERTS WOOD

November 4, 1911
At the Dawson's

Dearest Mama,

Katie running with the wrong crowd! I know how that must worry you. I remember Roland Mills, but not his mother nor that his grandfather had been a saloon keeper. If Katie goes to dances at the Millses', if these are properly chaperoned, I cannot think any harm can come from it. Mama, times do change, and you must change with them. Here, no one would think twice about someone's grandfather having been a saloon keeper. But I don't think Katie should ride the streetcar—ever. *Don't let her do that!*

This morning the Sullys drove over to take me to the Sunday morning services at the White Star Baptist church. When they arrived, the Dawsons, already in their wagon, were just leaving for an all-day singing and dinner on the ground. The men jumped out and shook hands, but the women remained seated as if already in church, Mrs. Sully's black silk bonnet nodding to Mrs. Dawson's brown cotton head-scarf, nodding slightly as a stranger might.

In church I was the only one wearing a leghorn hat, and this must have accounted for the open stares we received as we walked to the Sully pew. The church, a white clapboard square scarcely larger than the Sully dining room, seems much like ours at home with its "Onward Christian Soldiers" and "Just As I Am" sung robustly by the women but hesitatingly by the men, who seemed embarrassed by the emotional fervor with which their wives and sweethearts sang. The sermon was addressed mostly to the men, Brother Tinsley saying that if the men would only be righteous, the women would kneel at their feet.

After church we drove to the ranch for dinner. Mrs. Sully, still deeply mourning the loss of her youngest child, smiled only when Bob said that his two sisters, now attending school in the East, would be coming home for Christmas. Mr. Sully chuckled and said, in his deep gravelly voice, "This house will come alive then!"

Mama, I will not be coming home until Christmas. The little Baldridge twins missed a month of school when they had the whooping cough. Oda Ray has caught right up, but Ida Fay is still far behind, and a new teacher would not know how to work with her. She is shy and cries easily. She learns best at recess when we work quietly without the other students who would almost certainly laugh at her mistakes.

Love,
Lucy

November 5, 1911
At the Dawson's

Dear Diary,

Yesterday, a little war was declared. I'm almost sure of it.

Such a jumble of a day. Cold and cloudy but with no real promise of rain. Carlos was alone in the schoolyard as we drove off to the little church, so like the one at home I could have cried. And my visit to the Sully's only sharpened the pain.

When dinner was over, the men excused themselves to have a smoke, and the women went into the parlor.

There the silence, broken only by the occasional shifting of our bodies in the horsehair furniture and the crackle of burning wood in the fireplace, became almost too much to bear. I longed for the steady click of Aunt Catherine's needles and the sound of Mama's rich contralto voice at the piano. Then Mrs. Sully cleared her throat and asked, "What exactly did your father do?"

Grace Sully's "Why, Eleanor!" showed she was as shocked by the question as I.

I looked directly at her and said, "He was in the hardware business."

"And now? Your family?"

And again, incredulously, "Eleanor!" But Mrs. Sully's prying would not be stopped.

"Mama runs the business now," I said, pulling my shawl around my shoulders against the chill in her voice.

Mrs. Sully exchanged a look with her sister-in-law, a look that said as plainly as words could, "You see. I told you she was common."

My face flushed; I could feel it. "It's a new day for women," I said. "Why look at them all over the world. Back home, Mrs. Owens works in the bank with her husband on Saturdays, and Mrs. Tilson runs her husband's farm."

But, I might as well have been a telephone bird, chattering in the wind, for all she heard. Shortly afterwards, I asked Bob to take me home. When we were almost there, I said, "Bob, stop here a minute. Let's walk over to look at the river."

When he took my hand in his, the pain eased. We walked to its bank in a peaceful, comfortable silence and stood gazing at the river slowly flowing around the sand bars that look like little islands in the wide muddy water.

"In a way it's pretty," I said, but I wasn't thinking about the river. In spite of his mother, I have decided that one way or another Bob's ring will soon be on my finger.

Love,
Lucy

November 6, 1911
At the Dawson's

Dear Mr. Arnold,

How could I have thought I might leave my profession? Teaching gives me such pleasure, and today it gave me one of my richest moments, a moment I know you will want to share.

My three little first graders, the Baldridge twins and Peep Wilkins, had worked for weeks on their reading scrapbooks. We had cut brightly colored material into oblong squares, sewn eight of these together with a seam down the middle and folded them over to make three little cloth books with sixteen pages in each. Then we found pictures (the Baldridge twins liked those that represented the things they know—a churn, a hoe, a beautiful woman, elegantly dressed, who they say, with boundless love, looks just like "Ma," a grandmotherly woman who, I suppose, could resemble their Aunt Molly; Peep's is more exotic, with pictures of Eskimos, a python, and the Amazon River), pasted them in, and I printed appropriate words underneath the pictures.

The day was almost over, and we were finishing our reading lesson, reviewing Peep's book one last time. Of the older pupils, only Bucy Abernathy was paying attention to the reading, mouthing "elephant," "mountain," "ocean" as the little ones said the words aloud. I was watching Bucy's lips, enjoying the pride he took in his accomplishment, when I saw that Carlos, who had entered silently to remove the ashes from the woodstove, was reading right along with Bucy.

"Carlos," I said, "Why, you can read! You are learning to read!"

The children and I looked at him in astonishment.

I am very happy. The questions you asked the day Sheriff Ponder rode off without his prisoner, "What about Carlos? Who asked him?" have haunted me. Today I asked Carlos if he'd like to become a student in the White Star school. His brown eyes danced as he answered, softly, "Ye-es." So I have a new pupil, one so naturally intelligent that I believe he will soon outdistance even Bucy.

Still I wonder how he came to be here. Who is he? Where are those who love him, long to see him again?

Sincerely,
L. E. Richards

November 8, 1911
At the Dawson's

Dear Mr. Arnold,

I believe you do the people in the White Star community an injustice. Surely no one could deny a young boy, especially one who takes such pride in his job at the school, an education. I do not understand why you say the situation will alarm the community and is "not in my best interests." I would like to discuss this with you further.

Since you first described the singing at a brush arbor revival, I have wanted to attend one, and I shall be happy to go with you this Thursday evening. And then we can talk about Carlos.

Sincerely,
L. E. Richards

November 10, 1911
At the Dawson's

Dear Diary,

What am I going to do? Oh, my gosh! When Mama finds out I'm no longer a Methodist, it will just about kill her.

Last night at the brush arbor revival I joined the Church of the Everlasting Love. I did not intend to join. Lord knows I didn't. But the wind was ruffling Brother Arlington's black hair above his black eyes that looked right into mine—pleading, begging, calling me, just me, to come to Jesus, and the singing—the men's voices booming out, proudly, "There's uh wide-ness in Go-od's mer-cy, like the wide-ness of th-uh sea," and I could see the lights of White Star shining eleven miles away. In his sermon Brother Arlington talked about love and good-ness and time—about the quiet places in time and the surges in time, and his hands, as he spoke, followed flocks of birds in flight, herded schools of fish, and rocked the cradles of sleeping babes. He asked (and I was drown-ing in his eyes) those who wished to be baptized in the river on Sunday to "take one step as we sing 'Shall We Gather at the River,'" and the sweetness of it, those clear voices singing, just as Mr. Arnold had said they would, "Shall we gath-er at the ri-ver, the be-u-ti-ful, be-u-ti-fu-el ri-e-ver," and then Brother Arlington, crooning the words, "Just one step, oh, won't you take just one step tonight? If you have sinned this day or any other, won't you take one step?" and I took a step and "Hallelujah!" Brother Arlington shouted and then, still shouting, "If you want to go to heaven," bearing down hard on the "heaven," "if you want to come to love" and now leaning forward, his arms outstretched, his foot keeping time to the rhythm of his voice, "Oh, come to glory! Come!" and I was all the way down to the front, kneeling, feeling the touch of his hands on my head, only faintly hearing the "Amen's," "She's saved. It's the teacher and she's saved." The only one saved that night, I stood by Brother Arlington's side as the congregation sang "Turn, Sinners, Turn." Then they filed past, shaking my hand, squeezing my shoulders, hugging me, and I knew as I stood there, I had not been thinking about my sins at all when I walked to the front of the brush arbor revival, but about the swirling night and Brother Arlington's eyes and my hand in Bob's.

On the way home I did not say a word until Mr. Arnold laughed, and then I asked, "What's so funny?"

"Not a thing. Not one thing," he said, but he laughed again.

"Stop the motor car. I'll walk home," I said.

He stopped immediately and before I knew his intentions, he was kissing me, his mouth on mine with the same urgency that, a few minutes earlier, had been in Brother Arlington's voice, and, for a minute, I was drowning there too. Then I pushed him away, jumped out of the car and began to run.

"Lucinda," he shouted, "you're pretty, but I don't think I can wait for you to grow up."

This is *all* so embarrassing; I'll never go anywhere with Josh Arnold again. If I can get myself out of the

Church of the Everlasting Love and back to the Methodists, I'll never see Josh Arnold again.

Determinedly,
Lucy

P.S. We did not discuss Carlos at all.

November 10, 1911
At the Dawson's

Dear Brother Arlington,

I am sorry that I cannot be baptized on Sunday as I have a sore throat, and by November, Red River is already a little chilly.

From now on, I plan to attend regularly the Baptist church in White Star as it is more nearly like the Methodist Church to which I belong in Bonham.

Sincerely,
Lucinda Eliza Richards

November 10, 1911
At the Dawson's

Dear Lillian,

I know you are helping Mama all you can. She has her hands full with the hardware store and Aunt Catherine's erysipelas so bad this year. And Katie. What about Katie? Mama hints darkly that she is running with the wrong crowd and that everybody in Bonham is talking about her.

Is this so? What are they saying? *Is* Katie running wild or is Mama just old-fashioned? Please write me immediately, telling me everything.

Just yesterday Carlos told me he hoped his family

would come for him one day. He said that on the day Sheriff Ponder arrested him, his father and mother had gone with his younger brother and sister into Estelline to buy supplies, leaving Carlos at their campsite. He had walked over to Red River to try to catch some fish with a bent pin and a piece of string and was fishing about two miles down river from the campsite when Sheriff Ponder found him.

Today Carlos and I found the place where his family left him, and with flat, white rocks we wrote the name "Carlos" and then made an arrow pointing directly toward the schoolhouse.

In the spring, when his family begins their northward trek, they will surely be drawn once again to the place where they last saw their son. What a happy reunion that would be!

You ask if I still care for Bob Sully. Oh, Lillian! Care is not the word. I long to see him and (I write this only to you) to hold him in my arms. At times, this longing is so intense I could die.

Lovingly,
Lucy

November 11, 1911
At the Dawson's

Dear Diary,

A glorious Indian summer day. As warm as in June. I knew Bob would be riding over, knew before I looked out my window. My true love is coming, I whispered, my true love is coming! I ran to the window and there he was, the size of a chessboard knight, silhouetted against the pellucid blue of the prairie sky, unmistakably Bob, his right shoulder slightly raised by his right hand that carried the reins, Surprise's plumed tail arched triumphantly as they moved smoothly, soundlessly toward me.

I ran downstairs for a pitcher of water and took a bird bath in my room. Then I brushed my hair one hundred times, leaning way over so that it fell, thick and luxurious about my shoulders, and since it was a warm day, slipped on my cornflower blue cotton skirt and white, full-bodiced blouse, all the while hurrying, hurrying, so that by the time I heard Surprise's hoofbeats below, my shoes were almost buttoned, and I leaned out the window, calling "I'll be right down." (Bob does not come in the Dawson's house, both because he will not and they do not ask him.)

My hand was in his as we took the path, made visible by my comings and goings, toward the schoolhouse. Enjoying the easy silence that often falls between us, we walked through mesquite, startling a covey of chickadees, past a small carpet of wait-a-minute hovered over by a snake doctor, at times aimlessly darting about, now fixed, hovering in mid-air, its wings small chips of blue glass. At the schoolhouse we sat on the steps in the warm sunshine, and I leaned my head against his shoulder.

"I knew you'd be coming today," I said.

"Didn't come last Saturday," he said, his hand on my cheek, drawing my head close.

"Oh, but you wanted to," I cried.

"Yes, I did," and he grinned. "Mama kept me busy all day."

"Oh?"

"But today, this morning, I just rode off. I wanted to

see my girl," and he blushed but kept right on, "wanted to ask you to the Christmas party. It's five weeks off. Folks come from all over; some stay the week."

"Oh yes, I'll come," I said. "Of course, I'll come," and already I could see me, Lucinda, standing, no, *descending* the stairs of the Sully ranch house wearing a Christmas red dress with white, lace-trimmed petticoats peeping out beneath its full skirt. I'd ask Miss Elam to make the dress, and I'd write Maggie Owens tonight, "lord it over her a little."

But Bob's thoughts were on a different track, for he stood abruptly, gathered a handful of pebbles, and began chunking them one by one at a rusty Prince Albert can.

"Lucinda," he said, still focusing on the can, his words punctuated by the "ping," "chuff," "chuff," "ping" of his hits and misses, "folks are beginning to talk about you."

"What are they saying?" I asked, astonished by the sudden rush of anger I felt.

"That you'll teach anybody."

"I suppose they mean Carlos," I snapped.

"Suppose so."

"Anything else?"

Now he turned and looked at me, his eyes hurt and puzzled. "Folks say you're not spiritual-minded."

"Who says that?" and, suddenly, I was shouting. "Your spiritual-minded mother?"

He did not answer, but the blue of his eyes deepened and the pebbles fell from his hands as he clenched and unclenched his fists. Then he mounted Surprise and rode away. At the gate he turned Surprise; for just a minute, he turned him back, but then he spurred him into a lope.

60

Oh, I could bite off my tongue. Why do I have such a temper? Why am I so stupid? So mean and spiteful.

Afterwards, I cried, burying my face in H.H.'s fur that smells of sun and goodness and wind. And was a little comforted.

I love him more than anything.

Heartbroken,
Lucy

November 12, 1911
At the Dawson's

Dear Bob,

I am sorry I lost my temper when you came calling. There is no reason for this, nor is there an excuse. Please accept my apology.

However, I am not sorry to be teaching Carlos. His gentleness, his eagerness to learn, his quick understanding make him an excellent pupil, one that would gladden the heart of any teacher.

As to my spiritual-mindedness, I am not sure what is meant by this phrase. Perhaps we could discuss it calmly this coming Saturday afternoon. I'll bake some gingerbread, just in case you stop by.

Until Saturday,
Lucy

November 13, 1911
At the Dawson's

Dear Diary,

I do not understand these people. I will never understand them.

Last Monday, the wind was up, blowing hard enough to bring in a cold spell, but the schoolhouse (I love that little place), already warmed by the fire Carlos had made, was cozy and inviting. That morning, the Baldridge twins came giggling into the classroom carrying a wriggling bundle wrapped in three or four frayed and dirty quilts. As they unceremoniously began to unroll it, shake it out onto the floor, I thought it must be a stray dog they had found on the way to school, but when they stood back, smiling proudly, I saw it was a baby, a shy, fey creature with cotton hair and tiny tufts of white eyebrows above a wide, thin mouth, giving it the look of a little fox. Toddling around in a torn, faded pink dress, it held the children spellbound, and, at first, I too enjoyed the diversion.

"What's her name?" I asked.

At this the twins went into peals of laughter, fell down on the floor in their excitement and joy at the question, the others joining in their merriment.

"Name's Samuel," Oda Ray said. (Everybody in the Baldridge family has a biblical name except the twins because for them Mrs. Baldridge couldn't find two that rhymed). "He's a boy," this amidst another round of laughter, and now I too was laughing.

All day long the students, excited by the diversion, never settled down. As Baby Samuel aimlessly roamed about the room—deftly grabbing pencils from desks, sitting in Jessie Sams' lap and then (another round of laughter) leaving on Bucy's booted foot an unmistakable wetness—cried, slept, woke up and roamed again, the students never settled down.

On Wednesday, Bucy Abernathy brought *his* little sister, four years old, with him, and although Bucy was more responsible than the Baldridge twins, more aware that our work must not be interrupted, the presence of Baby Sister, for so she's called, made teaching difficult. Only Bucy's sweet smile and murmured, "Ma's sick and Pa had to go to town" caused me to allow her to stay.

At morning recess as I sat on the steps watching H.H. and the baby at play, Little 'Un Sams whispered in my ear, "Baby Sister has lice."

Horrified, I saw the resigned violence with which the baby scratched her head and, during arithmetic, became aware of Bucy's own furtive scratching. Then the room seemed filled with it, and *I* could not settle to my teaching, even once or twice yielding to a desperate urge to scratch my own head.

On Friday both Samuel and Baby Sister were back, along with two of the Sams' children and Jinks Mayfield's five-year-old cousin, visiting from Childress. Enough! I thought. Enough of minding all the babies in Hall County. My voice was shaking with anger as I ordered them all—the twins, Bucy, Big 'Un Sams, and Jinks to take the little ones home. "Take them right this minute," I said, trying to keep my voice even. "I am a teacher, and my business is to teach and yours is to learn. So take all these babies home. Now! At once!"

When the Baldridge twins protested that "Ma's working in the field with Pa," I shouted at them, shouted at two little lambs, "Well *you* stay home with Samuel then. Until your mother comes home, *you* take care of him. *I'm* going to teach an arithmetic lesson."

They were both crying pitifully, whimpering almost soundlessly, as they struggled into their coats, worn thin, and wrapped the baby up for the long walk home.

The rest of the day was spent in a room of silent, bewildered children, and today I had a letter from the trustees, asking me to appear before them on Monday.

This temper of mine will be the ruination of me. Mama has always said this, and I know she's right.

Lucy

November 14, 1911
At the Dawson's

Dear Bob,

The Board of Trustees has asked me to appear before them on Monday evening at 7:00. This meeting will be at the White Star Feed and Seed Store, and I would appreciate it if you would drive me there.

Lucy

November 17, 1911
At the Dawson's

Dear Bob,

No, I did not know Mr. Sully had gone to Chicago. You had not mentioned this to me. Still I do not understand your saying, "Pa will fix things when he returns." The problem seems so simple to me. I cannot teach *and* care for younger children at the same time. The community must decide if it wants a teacher or a nurse. I cannot be both. When I explain this to the trustees, who are reasonable men, the problem will be solved.

I will be ready at 6:00 on Monday.

Lucy

P.S. Oh, Bob, what has happened to us? You seemed so cold when I saw you last, even refusing a piece of hot gingerbread. And I always say too much, and you say almost nothing. Whatever happens on Monday will not affect our friendship. When you asked me to the dance, you said I was your girl. I still am . . .

Your girl,
Lucy

November 18, 1911
At the Dawson's

Dear Mama,

I have been so busy getting ready to move to the Constable's that I have not had time to write. However, I have finished the yellow curtains for the kitchen window, and you would be pleased at the evenness of my stitches. Mr. and Mrs. Dawson are going to be so surprised. I can hardly wait for them to see the soft jonquil yellow in their kitchen window.

Mama, I am proud of you. When some little thing goes wrong for me out here, I think of you. I say to myself, why if Mama can run the hardware store, I can surely do this.

I miss you, today more than most.

Love,
Lucy

November 18, 1911
At the Dawson's

Dear Mr. Arnold,

I appreciate your offer to provide transportation to the Board of Trustees' meeting on Monday night, but Mr. Sully already has arranged to drive me there.

I am surprised that you say my "predicament" has furnished entertainment for folks all the way from White Star to Childress. I hope these people will be just as entertained by the voice of sweet reason (my own), when I explain away my so-called "predicament."

You also write that in fights, West Texans are as liable to use buckshot as a single bullet. I appreciate your comment, but I plan to use a single bullet—my assurance that I am a good teacher.

Sincerely,
L. E. Richards

November 22, 1911
At the Dawson's

Dear Diary,

In bed three days with chills and fever. Bowels sickened, turned to water. Am able to keep down only a little red-oak bark tea. Whether sleeping or awake, the nightmarish meeting with the trustees last Monday haunts me. The specter of Mr. Sams—his shriveled prune of a face, scrawny arms resting upon his melon-shaped belly, his voice rasping out his unexpected and accusing question: "Miss Richards, don't your contract *that you signed* not state that you will regularly attend church here?"—rises before me again and again, sweeping away my logic, carefully prepared, which would have explained why the little ones cannot come to school. His voice overrides my whispered, "Yes," poking, probing, "And, Miss Richards, how many times have you attended?" His tobacco spittle hits the tin spittoon, contemptuously drowning out my answer, "Twice." Then Mr. Baldridge leans forward, cupping his ear, his fingers covered with long white hairs, demanding, "What?" and again my response, "Twice, just twice."

I have not recovered from Mr. Sams' questions when Mr. Baldridge takes over. Looking like a wizened Baby Samuel, but cunning and treacherous, all innocence gone, thrusting on the point of his finger the words toward me, he leans forward, "Miss Richards, in your classroom my girls study with a Mexican? Huh? That right? Huh?" I answer, hating the quiver in my voice, "Yes, all the students do." Then, fangs bared, snarling, "And do they study with a dog too? With a fancy no-account dog the Sullys give ye?" His anger crackles, whips snake-like into the room, and I silently implore Mr. Constable's help, but he sits, impassive, behind the scarred oak table, calmly whittling a piece of wood, whittling it away, until by the end of the meeting it is gone, a pile of curled shavings on the floor at his feet. Oh no, I think, I'll soon be living at your house, under your roof. Not you too. Why, I went down into the well for Squint, for your son. And now this? From you?

Suddenly, he clicks his knife shut, and softly, softly, but with no gentleness in the softness, says, "Mr. Baldridge, Mr. Sams, let's excuse Miss Richards for a few minutes while we talk this over privately," and so I wait outside, chilled to the bone, and Bob's "Don't worry, Lucy. Papa will fix it when he gets back," fails to reassure me.

It is Mr. Constable who calls me back, holds my chair as I sit down (his only kindness), then stands, his hands behind his back, looking at the curled shavings on the floor. "Miss Richards," he says, not *unkindly*, "we pay your salary. We do not pay you to teach Mexicans. If you stay on in this community, we expect you to teach *our* children and to attend church regularly. Any church.

The Baptist church right here in White Star or any of the other churches that regularly hold revivals out here." Then he adds, and, curiously, I imagine a smile, "I understand you've already taken an interest in one of these."

My mind swings loose, wheels far beyond the earthbound room toward the soft callings of wild geese, the whispered beating of their wings.

"Miss Richards?" comes Mr. Constable's voice again.

"I'd like to think it over," I say, finally.

"Think it over!" Mr. Baldridge shouts. "Tarnation! What's to think about?"

"Jim," says Mr. Constable, "Jim, that's her answer for now. She'll think it over," and I nod to the trustees and walk out into the cold.

Afterwards, as Bob cranked his car, Mr. Constable came out and got into Mr. Arnold's motor car, and the two drove off together. Then I understood Mr. Arnold's comment. The bullet of good teaching is no defense against the buckshot of prejudice.

Tomorrow I'll go to the schoolhouse, and if the children come, I will teach them. Beyond that I have not yet thought.

Mrs. Dawson has been exceedingly kind to me. This morning I told her Aunt Catherine always made chicken soup when any of us were sick, and just now the smell of it wafted up the stair. (I hope she did not kill one of her laying hens for it). More than that, when she came in a minute ago, H.H. was on the foot of my bed, and she did not say a word.

Weakly,
Lucy

THE TRAIN TO ESTELLINE

November 23, 1911
At the Dawson's

Dear Diary,

First day back at school. The children were subdued
with me and with each other, as if the events of the past
week had made strangers of us all. All morning I felt
such a roaring in my head and a tightness in my chest
that I had to force myself to stay behind my desk.

Just before recess, George Sams (I asked the children
to call "Big 'Un" and "Little 'Un" by their rightful names
because I believe a measure of dignity comes from a
name) announced, "A Sully's coming." I saw immediately that it was not Bob in the shiny, black buggy, and I
soon recognized the broader shoulders, the more an-
gular frame of his father. Mr. Sully tied the little roan to
one of the poplar trees, came in and sat down, dwarfing
the desk he chose. He motioned for me to continue the
math lesson, and when it was over, I shooed the children
from the room. After we had exchanged greetings, I sat
in a desk across from his, feeling strangely tired.

He looked out the window, running his fingers along
the crown of his wide-brimmed hat, and I saw that his
eyes are the same blue as Mrs. Sully's but something
. . . , I don't know what, the wrinkles around them, his
gray shaggy eyebrows—*something* gives his eyes an as-
pect of kindness. "Those trees out there," he said, "right
now they're too busy puttin' down roots to do much else,
but this spring, they will leaf out and grow. Be real pretty."

"We've watered them. Almost every day."

He nodded and then, more kindly than anyone had
spoken to me since I had left home, *more gently*, he said,
"Miss Lucy, what's this I hear about your giving these
folks out here a hard time?"

Unexpectedly, violently, I burst into tears. I put my head on my desk and sobbed. I cried because Papa was dead and so was Dickie Sully. I cried because I was so far from home. I cried because of the ugliness at the Dawson's and because of the hurt I still felt from the lash of Mr. Baldridge's anger. I cried because my head hurt and because I had lost my temper with the Baldridge twins.

Mr. Sully waited silently until the storm had passed, waited as if he sat by a weeping woman every day of his life. When it was over, although my headache was worse, for the first time in weeks, I felt sheltered. Home again.

"It's just that . . . ," I said, "it's just that, out here, everything is hard." And I began to weep again.

"Now, now, Miss Richards. Do you want to talk about this another day?" he asked.

I shook my head and went to my desk to get a handkerchief. "No, today. Let's talk about it today," I said and wiped the tears from my face and tucked the handkerchief into my sleeve, hearing Mama's voice, "A white handkerchief is the mark of a lady," feeling strengthened by it.

"Lucy," he said, using my given name for the first time, "the people out here are good folks. They mean well, but all that most of them have is a small piece of land to work. I've said for years this country's not for farming, but, poor fools, they keep trying. So they have a little land, a mean, little house, and—enormous pride. *Enormous* pride. And you've got to allow them that pride. Now, I could fix it so you'd have your job as long as you want it, but I can't make them accept you as a teacher. You've got to do that. Can't you back off a little? Go a little slower." He stood and walked to the door, watching the students at play. "Why, you're the only *real* teacher we've ever had out here. They know that. Just back off a little." Then he turned and, suddenly, was looking at me strangely. "Why, girl!" I heard him say as I stood up and then I was falling, falling . . . into blackness.

Mr. Sully brought me home in his buggy, and Mrs. Dawson put me to bed. Now if my chest will just stop hurting I am going to sleep and sleep and sleep.

Lucy

November 27, 1911
At the Constable's

Dear Diary,

First a voice bubbling out from the darkness. Too tired to open my eyes, I sleep. Then the voice again, like water, clear, spring water —lilting, bubbling, overflowing, "Drink this," and a cool hand under my neck holds my head. "Drink this. A little boneset tea will ease your throat." Sleep again, or almost sleep, still hanging on to the bell-like sounds, and after a while, "Now, Lucy Locket, here's a poultice. Let's just put," opening my gown, "the cheesecloth here!" and a huge white butterfly flutters gently to my chest, and then a heavy warmth that smells, not unpleasantly, of sweet field onions and mutton is placed over the white lightness.

I open my eyes, and it is night. Another poultice, this one of turpentine and wintergreen fern, is patted onto my chest. Giles Dawson's rooster crows, waking me, and I am looking into the strangest eyes I've ever seen— large green ones, the green of the irises rimmed inside and out with cobalt blue—eyes that look at me, through me, seeing into the center of things. Beyond the eyes, there is a large washtub, steam rising from it, on the stove, and I realize I am lying on a small bed in the Dawson's kitchen.

"Well, you've had a time of it." And hearing the bell-like voice, I lie there weakly, overwhelmed, feeling like some first human being, newborn. "Mr. Sully came for me four days ago, Lucy. I've been helping Mabel Dawson with the nursing. I'm Christobel. Christobel Constable."

"That ole fool of a doctor Mrs. Sully brought from Plainview near 'bout kilt you," says Mrs. Dawson, and I know that she too is in the room, moving to the cook stove, opening its door, stoking it, "but I said to Giles, 'If anybody can pull her through, Mrs. Constable here can,'" and turning, putting her hands on her hips, she beams, "And she did!"

Mrs. Constable holds my head while I sip a hot broth, thick like oatmeal, but not tasting at all like oatmeal. Then she moves over to a trunk ("It's rosewood," she said later), on the kitchen table, its lid open. "Some more heal-all," she says; "We need that, and some ginger root. There's plenty of wild cherry bark, and," opening a small leather pouch and shaking a red tinbox, "there's mullen root here."

"H.H.," I cry, suddenly longing to see him again.

"Why, honey, he's right by your bed, hasn't left your side a minute," and I drop my hand over the side of the bed onto H.H.'s head, feeling his muzzle, like velvet, his tongue in the palm of my hand.

"And there's someone else who's hardly left your side," says Mrs. Constable, and now the tears fall from the corners of my eyes. Such a crybaby I've become!

"Bob? Bob Sully," I say, overcome with joy.

"Bob's been here too. But Josh Arnold's hardly left the house, except for teaching and running back and forth between this house and mine, fetching remedies for you and changes of clothing for me. This morning I sent him off to Plainview for quinine and some tins of tomato juice. He'll be here again after his school's out."

Later in the morning, Mrs. Constable bathes me, Mrs. Dawson clucking her disapproval, brushes my hair, fluffs up the pillows behind me, and I sleep again.

Josh Arnold is there when I wake up, his mouth stern, his voice angry. "Lucinda, are you all right? Mrs. Constable, is she all right? Do you need anything else? Anything?" His energy exhausts me. "Lucy, are you feeling better now?" he asks roughly, and how easy it seems to close my eyes and drift away from the anger, the demands, the asking . . . what?

Dear Diary, it's been days since I've written you or anybody. Today, I have begun to write everything I remember. Tomorrow, I will write some more.

Lucy

November 29, 1911
At the Constable's

Dear Diary,

This is what else I remember.

Two days after I "returned to the world" as Mrs. Dawson said repeatedly, Bob Sully came for me in his handsome, new Pierce-Arrow saloon car, Christobel (Mrs. Constable has asked me to call her by her given name) having gone ahead to get my room ready. When I heard the motor of Bob's car, I handed the Dawsons the present I had made them.

"It's kitchen curtains," I said as Mrs. Dawson sat wordlessly, looking at the yellow spill of fabric in her lap. "I hope you like yellow."

"Oh, child" (calling *me* child!), "why they're the prettiest I've seen." Turning to Mr. Dawson, she added shyly, "We'll miss her, Giles. Won't we miss her?"

"Why, we'll even miss ole H.H.," said Mr. Dawson, and the two of them looked rather forlornly, or so it seemed to me, at each other.

When Bob and Mr. Dawson carried my trunk to the car, Mrs. Dawson holding the door open for them, suddenly, inexplicably, I slipped the tapeworm jar from the table and hid it under my cape. As Bob and I drove across the canyon, I asked him to stop in the middle of the bridge, and I threw the jar as far as I could down into the canyon.

These past days I've been strangely comforted by the thought of the yellow curtains hanging like splashes of soft sunlight at Mrs. Dawson's kitchen window, and I've hoped, I've *so* hoped, that in the evening she'll be sometimes at the window, with her hair falling to her waist, turning to smile at her husband when he comes in from the field.

Pleased,
Lucy

November 30, 1911
At the Constable's

Dear Mama,

I know you have been worried—not hearing from me. I am recovering from pneumonia, nursed back to health by Christobel Constable, who uses many of Aunt Catherine's remedies.

I realize I am much better today because almost for the first time since I became ill, I am fretful about my students. They have now missed eleven days of school, and as I am forbidden to leave the house this week, they will have missed sixteen days by the time I return. How will they ever catch up?

Mama, I am writing Katie a letter. Perhaps she will listen to her sister, one who is much older and wiser now than when she left home. But, Mama, do let her have a black dress for the Christmas ball. When I was her age, I would not have wanted one, but what harm is there in it? Times are changing, and we must change with them.

Just now Christobel swept my room with carbolic acid water, saying that if there were any germs, this would kill them. Now with all the germs dead or dying, all I have to do is recover my strength.

Love,
Lucy

November 30, 1911
At the Constable's

Dear Diary,

Mama thinks Katie is a little stubborn. If Mama only knew how Katie had behaved when I rode the streetcar with her last summer, she'd know what I know. Katie is the wildest girl in Bonham!

Katie had begged me to come with her. "Everybody's riding," she'd said. "You just see everybody."

"All right, I'll come," I told her. "We'll have a good time together."

As we went upstairs to dress, Katie sighed contentedly. "There's lots of boys that ride," she said. Then, looking like an angel in her white lawn dress, all white except for the sash of blue around her waist, she came in and sat on my bed. Delicately running her tongue over her lips, she said, "Lucy, I can introduce you to two new boys, in town for the summer."

"Katie, I'm leaving in three days," I said, hugging her. "But it will be fun to ride with you."

Feeling all corners and angles around her softness, I tried on my blue and white sailor, then the pale gray shirtwaist, before finally settling on my rose print.

A little after seven, we were at the corner, waiting. When the streetcar turned from Elm onto Main, "Here it comes," Katie whispered, in just the way she whispered as a little girl, her tongue darting over her lips, her hand squeezing mine as the circus band, rounding the corner, would strike up a march. Her glance would dismiss the clowns, tumbling dully along, and the trapeze artists, earthbound, out of their element. Even the elephant, ponderously moving its great bulk along, would fail to hold her interest. But when the tiger, sometimes roaring fiercely, was rolled by in its red-barred cage, she was breathless. "Oh, if he were to get out," she would say. "What would we *do* if he were to get out!" She would read the circus billboards for the sideshows. "There's a geek," she would whisper. "Oh, Lucy, let's go see the geek tonight!"

"Katie loves excitement," Mama would say wearily. "Why that child lives from one circus to the next."

Now, breathlessly, her hand squeezing mine, she whispered, "Here it comes, Lucy. Here's the streetcar!"

Before her foot was on the first step, "Come on back, Katie," a male voice called from the rear. "Hey, Katie, I'm saving you a seat." And another, "Who's that you got with you?" "That's her sister, you dope. She's gonna be a teacher," and before I found his face, I recognized the voice of Maggie Owen's little brother.

As I followed Katie to the last seat on the car, a crescendo of male voices rose around us.

"Hey Katie, sit by me." "Aw Katie, I've been saving this seat for you." "You're looking real pretty tonight, Katie."

Smiling, Katie chose a seat, and with a wave of her hand and a "Charlie, please," cleared a place for me to sit. We rode past blocks of wooden houses—narrow, two-storied ones with gables and turrets, single-storied clapboards with wrap-around porches and gingerbread trim—all sitting comfortably behind lush, green lawns; then past the Methodist church, Mr. Coleman's blacksmith shop, Crawford's Dry Goods Store, Clutter Grocery, the Baptist church, Higginbotham Lumber Company, our own Richards' Hardware store (est. 1890), and the train station. Then the houses were further and further apart until we arrived at the streetcar yards. After five minutes, the streetcar turned around and started back down the other side of the street; Wise Funeral Parlor, Fannie Brice—Fine Milliner, Bonham High School, the courthouse, the post office, the city park, the fire station, the Willow Wild Cemetery, more houses, and, finally, the Rest in Glory Cemetery right at the edge of colored town. Twenty minutes from one end of town to the other; three times past our house in a little more than an hour.

Katie, smiling below her fringed lashes, her face flushed, her nose pink as if she had just come in from the cold, looked down, saying nothing at all. The young men, in their long-sleeved summer shirts of tan and blue and white, clustered around her like moths at a light, coming close, falling away, struggling back to meet her eyes, receive her smile, feel her finger tips against a wrist or in the palm of a hand, as all the while she silently said, "It's you." "It's you," her eyes, darting over this one's face, said, and, "It's you," the soft contour of her neck said as she swept her hair up into a honeyed cluster at the top of her head. "I want you," her fingers said against a frenzied brow, said to this one leaning over her shoulder, or that one at her side.

She seemed not to hear my, "Katie, let's go home," or, "Katie, whether you come or not, I'm getting off the bus when it passes our corner." "Katie, let's go home," I said again, but all at once we were at the car yard, and Katie was off the car and running, followed by Steve with the red hair and redder suspenders, running across the pasture into the gathering darkness.

The expression on my face stopped the grin that was spreading across the conductor's face.

"Miss, you afraid to walk home?"

"Not at all," I answered.

"Sure you don't want me to walk along with you?"

"I'm not at all afraid," I said loftily. "Not at all."

Long after I heard Katie's light foot on the stairs, followed by the quiet creak of her bed as she eased into it, I lay awake. Katie goes too far, I thought miserably.

That morning, I stayed in bed. I did not want to see Katie. I was glad to be leaving.

Now, so far away, I wonder if anything I might say in a letter to Katie would have the slightest effect on her. I doubt it. But I have promised Mama, and I will write the letter.

Lucy

December 1, 1911
At the Constable's

Dear Katie,

Please know I write this out of love for you *and* Mama.

In three days you will be seventeen, the age I was when I left home. Oh, Katie! I was sure that this would be my great adventure, and in some ways, it has been that. But the best times, the shining moments, have come as a result of just plain hard work.

Until you marry, focus on one of the professions (teaching or nursing), work hard, and you will experience the satisfaction that comes when one does a job well.

Lovingly,
Lucy

P.S. I wrote Mama that I hoped she would let you have a black dress for the Christmas ball. When I was your age, I would not have wanted black, but, as I reminded Mama, times are changing.

P.S. Again, I miss you very much.

December 2, 1911
At the Constable's

Dearest Lillian,

Your black silk umbrella burned in a grass fire? I know Edmund was disturbed when Katie came bringing just the blackened ivory handle back to you.

We must get Katie away from Bonham. If she could come out here for a while, she would, at least, escape her reputation. If she doesn't change soon, I hate to think what might happen to her.

I am feeling stronger every day, and recovering at the Constables is bliss. The house, weathered to a silver gray, sprawls haphazardly across the crest of a long, gentle incline. The rooms are filled with music—a victrola in the front parlor, a caged mockingbird (Christobel is wonderful with wild creatures), recovered from a broken wing, sings its heart out in my room, and the sound of Christobel's voice, like a fresh water spring, flows all through the house.

H.H., knowing I'm wonderfully taken care of here, comes and goes as he pleases, disappearing for hours and then trotting into my room as if to say, "Ah, there you are, doing just fine, as I knew you would be."

The first two days I was here I was not allowed visitors, but since then I have come to know the entire household. The first ones to come were Petey and Squint, Squint smiling broadly and Petey ducking his head in embarrassment. How happy I was to see them again! They share a room next to mine. That afternoon Amanda and Amy, who share a room on the other side of mine, the only girls still at home, came "just for a minute" to sit on my bed. They regaled me with stories of their older sister, Susan, a young bride who lives in the "weaning house" on the Constable farm, a small house the couple will live in until they can have their own place. The older sons sleep in a bunkhouse out in back.

The third evening I was allowed to come to the table, and I met the eldest son, Jonathan, small and wiry like his father, and Cable, by far the handsomest with his wide smile, dark blue eyes a little like his mother's, and black hair. The third one, Lacey, is too tall and slender to be considered attractive, but he exudes an air of preoccupied kindness.

Mr. Constable came in late. "Been talking to the Professor," he said, and nodding, "Miss Richards, we're glad to have you here." The talk at the table was of weaning calves, breaking land, and the railroad. Amanda and Amy served the meal, and when it was over, Mr. Constable took his wife's hand, and they went outside for a stroll. Then the seven children, each one apparently responsible for a task, washed, dried, and put away the dishes, fed the animals the kitchen scraps (H.H. loves the food), and swept and mopped the floors—all without a word of disagreement.

They firmly refused my offers to help, but of course I will do my part when I'm stronger.

Tomorrow I shall plan my school work for the following week. I am eager to be in the classroom again.

Love,
Lucy

December 2, 1911
At the Constable's

Dear Diary,

Only to you can I write freely and openly. What would it be like to have a sweetheart or even a friend with whom I could share my world, my entire world, instead of the bits and pieces I now share with my family and friends? Not even to Bob can I express my deepest concerns, my strongest feelings, but I know the day will come when our worlds will merge, become one.

Mr. Sully's advice to "back off a little" and "to allow them their pride" puzzles me, but I am beginning to *feel* a little of what he meant. I must think about how to allow the parents of my students their pride, and at the same time, do what is right. How can I "back off a little" from the teaching of Carlos?

Going to church is all right. It's in my contract, and I promised Mama I would go. But I must continue to teach Carlos. Although Mr. Constable has not yet mentioned the trustees' demands (the memory of that meeting is agony for me), I feel sure he will soon grow impatient for my answer.

Josh Arnold could help me. He knows these people, knows how they think, but I am determined never to ask his help again. Every problem I have becomes a source of amusement to him; I will work this out myself.

After I solve this dilemma, I have the most delicious plan for the future. When I marry Bob Sully, my teaching position at White Star will be vacant, and I shall see that Katie fills it.

On Saturday of this week, the Constable's closest friend, a professor, is coming to supper. Everybody seems to like him, and I am looking forward to meeting him.

Lucy

December 3, 1911
At the Constable's

Dear Diary,

After supper tonight I found myself alone in the front parlor with Mr. Constable, Christobel having gone out into the field with her butterfly net to catch a grasshopper for the mockingbird that, she says worriedly, "seems to be making no progress at all." The house was quieter than usual, and I could hear the sound of the windmill, its easy commitment to the wind that blows through it making it the most consoling sound in the world. Gathering courage somehow (I cannot explain it), from the sound, leaning forward so I could see his face, I whis-

THE TRAIN TO ESTELLINE

pered, "Mr. Constable, I'll go to church. It's in my contract and I'll go."

As startled as I by my whisper, unprepared for the subject, perhaps, he did not answer for a long minute. Then, "Lucy," and he sounded embarrassed, "we've always put that in the contract, that the teacher will go to church, but Christobel thinks we ought to take it out. She says that's not the school's business."

Now I felt magnanimous. "Oh, that's all right," I said. "I promised Mama I'd go, and I don't mind it."

"Well then, I think you and I—the Board—we see eye-to-eye. Well now. That's all worked out." He smiled at me, relighting his cigar with such good humor I could hardly force myself to continue.

"But I have to teach Carlos," and the whisper in my voice was there again.

"Christobel and I have worried some over that too, but," his voice, at first tenuous, now sounded angry, "out here Mexicans don't go to school. And that's final!"

"I have to teach him," I repeated, and I knew I'd never find the words to say why.

"Well, then. I just don't see any way out of this," Mr. Constable said. "You're a mite—Petey and Squint, now this is not your affair!" and only then was I aware they had been listening outside the door, "stubborn!" he finished.

"Mr. Constable, if you just knew him, you'd see that he's just like Petey or Squint . . . anybody. Why when he reads . . ."

"He's not like any of mine. I know that for sure!"

As calmly as I could, I said goodnight, angry at Mr. Constable, angrier still at myself because I could not find the words that would pierce his certainties. When I was halfway down the hall, he said, holding out an olive branch of sorts, "When the professor comes on Saturday, I'll talk it over with him. He'll have the answer!"

I imagine his friend will have the answer, but it will be Mr. Constable's answer.

Almost defeated,
Lucy

December 4, 1911
At the Constable's

Dear Bob,

Yes! Yes! Come over on Saturday evening! The Constables have a victrola in their front parlor. Wouldn't it be grand to waltz around and around in each other's arms?

Will there be dancing at your party? I hadn't thought to ask.

Until Saturday,
Lucy

December 6, 1911
At the Constable's

Dear Aunt Catherine,

Christobel has a new bird's-eye maple sewing machine, and we are going to make my dress for the Sully's Christmas party. I have sketched the design and will do all the handwork. She will run the machine because she says the violent pedaling is not good for a young woman's female organs.

I told her about your terrible trouble with erysipelas. She suggested that you make a poultice of corn meal and dried peach leaves. This, she said, would not only bring it to a head, but would also reduce the scarring which usually follows the infection.

Christobel has to be careful about wishing for something. When she does, either Mr. Constable or one of the boys gets it for her. That's how she got the machine.

Love,
Lucy

December 8, 1911
At the Constable's

Dear Diary,

It was the coldest day we'd had all year. The frost on the ground that morning was still there at sunset. I had almost finished dressing when I heard the hollow sound a motor car makes crossing the canyon bridges on its way to the Constables. Ran to the window. Surprised to see Josh Arnold's car as he stopped to open the pasture gate. Then Amanda and Amy rushed past my door, whipping off their aprons, calling out, "Christobel! Papa! Lucy! The Professor's here!"

I was glad my own room allowed me the privacy I needed to recover from the shock of realizing that the Professor and Josh Arnold are the same! How could I not have guessed? I am so stupid! But in the week I've been here not once have I heard him called by his rightful name. As I slipped into my blue gabardine skirt and sailor blouse, my image of a gray-headed, distinguished-looking man walking, probably with the help of an ivory-tipped cane, fell away. Josh? The Professor? Mr. Constable talking over my affairs with him? I hated the idea. But that he was once again involved in my affairs became immediately apparent. When I passed the closed doors of the parlor, I heard the almost inaudible murmur of his voice, along with Mr. Constable's, broken almost at once by his rollicking laughter. That laugh, rife with noisy humor, signaled that once again he was finding my discomfort amusing, and the thought propelled me back down the hall and, without knocking, through the parlor doors.

"Ah, Lucy, uh, Miss Richards," Josh said, standing, recovering from the suddenness of the interruption more quickly than Mr. Constable, whose teeth remained firmly clamped on his pipe. Then he too rose slowly to his feet.

"Lucy, I think we've worked this out fair for everybody," Mr. Constable said. "Josh, tell her about it while I go find Christobel. She'll be late for supper, and we've a good one tonight. The girls have baked your favorite cobbler."

Hearing the slam of the front door, then Mr. Constable's voice calling his wife, "Christobel, Chris-to-bel," the wind picking up the sound and carrying it off down the pasture, I looked at Josh and smiled.

"Ah, Lucy," he said, stepping forward, and his rough face, smelling of tobacco and carelessness and of something crushed—wild horsemint leaves?—was against mine, his lips on mine and, rising from the depths a sweet, strange urgency so that I opened my mouth to the warmth of his, and . . . "Don't ever let a man put his hands on you!" came the sound of Mama's voice, and I pushed him away.

"Josh! Don't!"

"You enjoyed it. Oh, girl. You're sweet!" he whispered.

The blaze in his eyes, the urgency in his voice, frightened me, calling up all the things I'd been told not to do. "Josh, stop it!" I said, again pushing him away. "Bob Sully's coming over tonight."

"Why that . . . !"

"He'll be over right after supper."

"Then, well then," and for a minute I was hurt by the sudden harshness in his voice, "let's get back to the business with the school. Mr. Constable says . . ."

"I intend to teach Carlos," I interrupted, welcoming his harshness, answering it with my own. "If I stay here, I am going to teach him."

"Well, look, tiger," he said, "simmer down. All you need do is write the trustees a letter saying you intend to go to church *and* you fully understand you are not paid to teach Carlos. Then mention that since you'll not be teaching him, he will have to be paid. If they pay him (I don't think they will), you can tutor him after school. If they won't, you can offer to pay him with your teaching."

"You make it sound so easy. I don't think it's that simple. Why Mr. Baldridge . . ."

"Forget Mr. Baldridge," Josh said. "His quarrel is with the Sullys. He hates them. He tried to get at them through you."

"Why?"

"Lucy, when the railroad came through here, those Yankees laid the tracks right through the farms. Didn't ask anybody. Just came right through. And now they charge outlandish prices to take these poor farmers' crops to market. It's highway robbery."

"That doesn't explain Mr. Baldridge's anger at the Sullys," I said.

Now Josh's words flew into the room so thick and fast that I only half-listened to what he was saying. It was impossible to know whether his anger was meant for me or for the railroad.

"Lucy," he said impatiently, "it's a fact that even a man as highly placed as our own Senator accepted money from the railroad. And Sully may have bought off the railroad. Baldridge thinks he did. But for whatever reason, the railroad just skirted Sully's ranch, and, in doing that, it went through a water tank on Baldridge's place. And about once a month, the train hits some poor soul's cow. Then folks get all stirred up again, mad at the railroad. Everybody but Baldridge. He gets mad at Sully."

I put my hand on his arm. "Josh, do you think . . . ?"

His touch was easy as he carefully, deliberately, as if a sudden movement would break it, took my hand from his arm and let it fall to my side, but his voice was just as angry. "Look, Lucy. Folks are saying that if they can just get you back in the classroom, they will even pay you to teach H.H. You look half-starved, you have a terrible temper, but by God you're a good teacher!"

He turned and was gone. I stood there, leaning against the doors, enjoying the sudden rush of happiness I felt. I'm a good teacher, I said to myself. By golly, I'm a good teacher! I whirled across the parlor floor out of the sheer joy of thinking it.

Love,
Lucy

P.S. The strangest thing! Josh Arnold opened the doors to leave but then closed them again and said, "Lucy, better keep a lock on your trunk while you're here!" What can he have meant? Isn't that strange?

THE TRAIN TO ESTELLINE

Dear Maggie,

Your sweet, dear letter arrived this week. There is no reason to worry about me because I feel almost as strong as ever, and I have never been quite so contented. Maggie, dear Maggie, after a serious illness is one so easily made happy? Let me tell you about the events of yesterday.

Amanda and Amy Constable (I adore this family!), baked all morning, leaving just the fried chicken and the blackberry cobbler for the afternoon. I was given the easiest tasks—churning, dusting, setting the long oak table with blue stoneware. Although Christobel (even her children call their mother by her given name) was in the canyon looking for poke root for sciatica, the Constable men were there, almost underfoot, carrying water, bringing in wood, stoking the fires. The two youngest, Petey and Squint, washed up the stove vessels as they were used.

Josh Arnold arrived on time for the usual five o'clock Constable supper, and made me happy by saying, "By God! You're a good teacher." I was inordinately pleased by his remark, because, although we are not at all alike, he is the smartest man I've ever met, next to Bob, of course.

After supper, the Constable family shoved me out of the kitchen. I threw my red cloak around my shoulders and went outside to wait for Bob. Just at sunset, I heard his automobile on the canyon bridge and ran to open the pasture gate for him. He stepped from his motorcar wearing black silver-toed boots with the Sully brand tooled above the silver and a soft doeskin coat. As I walked beside him up the steps and across the front porch, I thought he was the handsomest man I'd ever seen.

The victrola was playing "Faded Flowers" when we went into the parlor. Then Squint played "May I Sleep in Your Barn Tonight, Mister," and Mr. Constable and Christobel danced together as smoothly as if they had been on ice. At the end of the dance, he kissed her on the lips right in front of us all. Then Josh danced with Christobel, and I danced with Cable, who is almost as handsome as Bob. When I rejoined Bob, he confessed he had never learned to dance, and Amy, overhearing this, immediately pulled him onto the dance floor.

Just as they do in Bonham, the men disappeared from time to time, and each time they reappeared, the effects of hard drink became more apparent. Squint and Petey pushed the furniture back and soon everybody, with or without partners, was dancing. Cable danced an impromptu Highland Fling to "Coming' Through the Rye," and when Squint played "When Irish Eyes Are Smiling," I was unable to contain the sheer joy I felt, so I danced by myself until Cable and Jonathan made a pack seat with their hands, swept me up, and danced me across the room.

The only unpleasantness of the evening came when we, all of us except Mr. Constable, went outside at ten to watch the train come through. (Twice a week one of the Constables has to be sure none of the cows are on the track and that the gates are opened and closed as the train crosses their farm). Bob Sully smiled when he saw it coming. "Right soon it will be taking our cattle past Fort Worth to Dodge," he said.

"Why you son of a bitch," Josh said, lashing out at him. "With ranches across five counties and the railroad just skirtin' your land!"

Christobel quickly took his arm. "Josh," she said. "Now, Josh! Bob Sully's company in this house," and they walked on back to the house.

Bob was too angry to come back inside, and we watched the train together. As the passenger car went slowly by, I could see faces looking out into the blackness of the night. It seemed strange to think they did not know I was there, holding Bob's arm and wishing we were on the train.

I asked Bob why his remark about the railroad taking the Sully cattle to market made Josh so angry. He said he guessed it was because the railroad had taken land from just about everybody in West Texas but his family.

"That's unfair," I told him. "And, anyway, I don't believe it!"

He didn't answer, but his hand on my arm tightened, and I could feel the anger there. I decided to switch to a pleasanter subject. "Bob," I said, "women will soon have the vote, and I can't wait. Just think! You and I could walk in together and vote for Mr. Wilson."

But it wasn't a better subject after all. Bob just stood there for a minute, shaking his head. Then he said, "Lucy, for God's sakes, don't mention Mr. Wilson's name to Pa, and I wish you'd keep quiet about women voting too. Mama's dead-set against that!"

I started to waltz right into the house, but the stars were swirling around, and I was cold. I decided I'd rather be kissed.

That was my second kiss of the evening.

Love,
Lucy
P.S. Women should have the vote. The sooner the better!

December 9, 1911
At the Constable's

Dear Diary,

Out here there's a moment! The sun drops below the horizon and, at once, the western sky is filled with oranges and reds and blazing pinks that gently, like a wide benediction, fade into violets, mauves, amethysts —light washes of color. And the wind, just as the colors begin to soften, usually dies away, and then I am at peace with the world but, at the same time, filled with a longing so intense it hurts my heart. But strangely, I do not know what I long for.

Lucy

December 10, 1911
At the Constable's

Dear Mama,

Today was a December Valentine. It was my first day back at school and never have I felt such affection. It came from all my students, every one of them there waiting for me, when Squint, Petey, and I drove up in the wagon. They gathered around, politely pushing each other out of the way, to help me down, hold my hands, touch my arms. Clucking like a mother hen with her chickens, I made my way into the schoolhouse and on my desk found a wonderful quilt. Called a friendship quilt, every person in the community has a square in it, embroidered with his name. Most of my students, even the youngest, made one, and for those too little to sew, the squares were made by their mothers or older sisters. A yellow water pitcher I recognized as Mrs. Dawson's was on my desk, filled with white branches hanging low with clusters of purple berries. Carlos, I believe, was happiest of all. Big boy that he is, his eyes filled with tears as he called out, "Teacher! Teacher! Look! Look!" and pulling me away from the quilt, he showed me his gift—a room sparkling clean, smelling of lye soap and vinegar water.

But oh, Mama, how cruel winter seems to me tonight. Today at school I stupidly told Berl to wear a coat these cold days, and there was an embarrassed silence until Peep Wilkins said, "He ain't got one," and Berl growled, "Shut up, Peep." The Baldridge twins came bringing a sweet potato hot from the oven because, as they cheerfully explained, it keeps their hands warm on the way to school, and a little later, it becomes their lunch. Only the Constables and I have adequate clothes and generous lunches.

Please ask at church for warm clothing—hats, scarves, coats, shoes, *especially* shoes—and send a box out here as soon as possible. It will soon snow and then, unless my students have warmer clothes, school will be impossible for them. When the clothes arrive, I'll somehow find a way around their ridiculous pride so they can accept them and continue their schooling.

Mama, I know Katie broke your heart when she said she was going to live with the Millses. She will soon tire of that fast life and come home again. Don't worry. I'll soon find a way for her to come out here.

And I want a piano for the school.

Love,
Lucy

December 11, 1911
At the Constable's
Dear Aunt Catherine,

I hate to tell you this, but almost every one of my students now has head lice. I think the infestation came from the Baldridge family. Mr. Baldridge is a school trustee, a very hot-tempered one.

Is there an unobtrusive way of getting rid of this problem? I'm afraid to touch the students, and when my head itches, it scares me to death. I remember that when I was in the first grade, Mary Cokewood was found to have head lice, and her hair was shingled so close she had to wear a scarf for the rest of the year. I live in terror of this.

Love,
Lucy

December 16, 1911
At the Constable's
Dearest Lillian,

Your shocking news came yesterday. Katie seems deliberately to be causing grief to her family. Coming to church with her hair bobbed! What must our friends have thought? Katie's beautiful, blonde hair on the floor of the barber shop! I cannot even imagine going into a barber shop. But Lillian, there is some part of me that envies her that courage. Wouldn't it be marvelous not to care what Bonham thinks? Or anybody?

All the "don'ts" we grew up with—don't trust a man who doesn't wear a hat; don't look in the barber shop when you walk downtown; don't cross your legs in pub-

lic; don't sit in a chair a man's just gotten up from —
seem unimportant out here.

But never mind all that. I'm so happy about Christmas, and Josh Arnold is the reason for it. Although he
and I have had our differences, I decided it would be
better if we could be friends. He is often at the Constable's, and they, every one of them, speak of him with
admiration and respect. So on Saturday morning, when
Josh stopped by, I made every effort to be friendly. I sat
for a while as he and Mr. Constable discussed the railroad. Mr. Constable bitterly resents it, dislikes the Yankees who brought it here, berates the railway men for
their carelessness with gates and cattle on the track. He
said, "Why those sons of bitches! Excuse me, Miss Lucy,"
and his face was red with anger, "the prices they charge!
It's highway robbery!"

Josh told him that since the railroads are somewhat
regulated now, the Easterners can't be so high-handed.
Then the two of them walked down to the lower field that
Cable and Jonathan were readying for spring planting.

The middle of the morning, I was drawing water
for the Saturday wash when Josh, who by then had vis-
ited everyone in the Constable family, wandered out to
the well.

"Let me do that, Lucy." he said, and I stood back,
watching him draw up bucket after bucket of water,
splashing each into the washtub I had brought from
the house.

"Christobel told me you want a Christmas tree for the
schoolhouse," he said when he had filled the tub.

"Oh, I do. Why some of the White Star children have
never seen a real tree," I said, and the remembered smell
of pine and fir sliced through the acrid odor of the rag-

weed that grows in clumps all around the well. "If we only had a tree. And a piano!" I added.

Josh threw back his head, laughing, and the sound was not unpleasant. "Good Lord, Lucy! These people don't have enough food to eat, they're parching corn to use for coffee, and you want them to buy a piano! How in the world can they do that?"

"A tree then. I'd settle for a tree," and I looked across the pasture at the thinly-branched mesquite, thought of the scrub oak growing down the canyon walls, and knew there was nothing out here that would reach even half-way up to the ceiling.

"Lucy, you come with me. Come on," and his smile was contagious. "I'll find you a tree." As I hesitated, thinking of the wash, knowing Bob would be coming that evening, he said, "Come on, Lucinda. Get in the car, and we'll drive until we find the prettiest tree in Hall County."

Enticed by his smile, beguiled by the idea of a tree, I ran to get my cloak, and by the time I reached the car, he had already cranked it and was waiting to help me in. When we reached the middle of the canyon bridge he stopped the car and we looked down, down into the dry canyon dotted with oak which, from the bridge, looked like small green balls. "See anything?" he asked.

"Josh, a Christmas tree should reach the ceiling," I said, shaking my head. "Those scrub oaks are only about three feet tall."

"We'll find a tall one," he said, smiling. "If it's a tall one you want, we'll find it!" (I don't know what makes his smile so nice except that his teeth are unusually white against his dark skin.)

When we reached the fence line of the Constable

farm, he stopped again. "Lucy, I think we've found our tree," he said, but I saw nothing more than a fence piled high with tumbleweeds.

Lillian, these grow everywhere out here. Green in the summer, they turn a silvery gray after the first frost, then break off, and are tumbled by the wind for miles across the prairie until they are stopped by some stationary object, usually a fence. At recess, my students and I sometimes race the tumbleweeds, or run to grab them from the wind.

Josh plucked from the fence a car full of the biggest tumbleweeds, and we drove to the schoolhouse.

"Lucy, in ten minutes you will have the tallest tree in West Texas," he said.

And in less than that, Josh had fashioned a tree as delicate as a spider's web, the tumbleweeds' fine network of branches holding them, however they were placed, together. He worked until the tree was taller than he could reach and, standing on a chair, he placed a perfectly round ball of a tumbleweed at its very top.

"Now," he said when he'd finished, "it needs—what does it need?" And I laughed at the perplexity in his voice.

Caught up in his excitement, I said, "Why, cranberries and popcorn. It needs color!"

"Berries! Let's go find some berries," he said, and we walked over to the river. There we found, not red, but berries silvered purple, and pale green, and white— enough for lavish garlands for the tree. And after dinner, Christobel, digging around in her ribbon box, found a spool of green plaid ribbon, enough for two dozen bows for the tree.

Now I cannot wait until Monday. The students will be so happy.

If we just had a piano, what a splendid Christmas it would be.

Love,
Lucy

December 17, 1911
At the Constable's

Dear Diary,

Grandmother's silver mesh purse has disappeared from my trunk, along with my white China silk shawl. My two prettiest things—gone. Josh told me to keep my trunk locked, and I should have listened.

To mention this to anyone would be to accuse someone of thievery. The idea that anyone here is dishonest is absurd. I will not believe it.

Still, from now on, I will lock my trunk and my diary in it!

Puzzled,
Lucy

December 18, 1911
At the Constable's

Dear Aunt Catherine,

When I got home from school today, there on my bed was the material for my Christmas dress. Christobel had driven into town with Mr. Sully and picked it up for me at the post office. Neiman-Marcus in Dallas was out of red velvet, and they sent blue instead, a blue the color of the West Texas sky, sparkling clear. After supper, we began on it immediately. Christobel cut it out and began sewing it on her machine, the fabric coming together like magic, the stitches small and even. But if you get one, be careful with it. I was holding the velvet while she pedaled when her red-tailed hawk cried out, and, startled by its call, she ran the needle through my finger. It is not so painful now as Christobel poured kerosene oil over it and then made a poultice of biscuit dough mixed with sugar and turpentine.

This evening, I will begin the handwork on the dress. It is designed to fall slightly off the shoulders with a tight waist and a full skirt. Christobel has a cream-colored lace collar she is letting me borrow, and I'll baste that on last. And she says the blue is prettier with my auburn hair than the red would have been. I think she is right.

Aunt Catherine, I told her about the lice. She says Mr. Constable will take it up at the next trustee meeting. If something is not done about it soon, I will have to take matters in hand. Christobel says the only way to get rid of lice is to wash every head with lye soap and fumigate the school with sulphur.

Love,
Lucy

December 19, 1911
At the Constable's

Dear Mama,

We have a piano! At the school! On Monday morning, Carlos came running to meet me. Too excited to speak, he could only point. A piano stood in the school yard under the poplar trees, looking as if it had been wafted there by a magician.

Oh, the joy of it! Squint, Petey, Carlos and I somehow

got it up the steps and into the schoolhouse, and I sat right down and began to play "Joy to the World!" As the students arrived, I laughed to see the looks on their faces. Baby Jesus in the manger could not have received more wondrous looks than that piano.

Mr. Sully is obviously the one who presented it to the school. When Mr. Sully drove Christobel home the other day, I told him about our Christmas tree and mentioned our need for a piano. Since he obviously wants his generosity to go unrecognized, I will keep his secret, but oh how I long to thank this good, kind man.

Now we'll practice our Christmas carols, and I'll ask all the families to come to the school next Monday for a Christmas caroling.

Thank goodness Katie has come home! You were right to allow her to have a black dress for the Christmas ball. And never mind what Mrs. Owens said about willful girls. Her own Maggie's just as headstrong. One day she just might decide to run away to Oklahoma to marry George. I do wish he would write Maggie. She is crazy about him.

Love,
Lucy

December 20, 1911
At the Constable's

Dear Maggie,

Never have I known a family like the Constables, coming and going all night long, the men anyway. At first I asked about it. "It sounded as if someone came in late last night," I'd say at breakfast, and Cable (oh Maggie, he's a handsome man), laughing, "Yeah, Lacey, why don't you tell us about her?" or Jonathan, shyly, "Cable, how late was that poker game?" Mr. Constable usually takes no notice of the teasing, but once he said, "It doesn't matter how late you boys stay out as long as you get to the field by the time I do." So accustomed have I become to these night prowlings that when I hear a hoofbeat at midnight or a door closing before sunup, I just turn over and go back to sleep.

In the daytime, the Constable women hurry about—cooking, cleaning, washing—all this with endless good humor. Their mother, Christobel, clearly the center of the household, yet somehow above it, heals. She heals birds, rabbits, ground squirrels, cows, calves, horses, people. She can get rid of warts, stop the hiccups or a nosebleed, break a fever, and cure erysipelas, coughs, and the seven-year-itch. She works with such calmness and certainty that when she comes into a sick room, turns a pillow, smooths a forehead, her patient feels immediately better. People say that she just holds out her hands when a woman's in labor, and the baby comes as easy as the sixth kitten of a litter. I do believe she saved my life when I had pneumonia.

They are outgoing and affectionate. If I sit by Christobel, she pats my arm or rubs my back as we talk. The older men treat me just as they do their sisters, and I am becoming quite used to being hugged and patted—or flipped with a cuptowel.

But one thing I cannot get used to is the camaraderie of the privy. Theirs, with four seats, is larger than the school's, and the first time I heard a male voice calling from the other side, "That you, Amy?" I almost fell in. I do not take part in the little morning visits with whoever happens to be on the other side.

Of them all, only Mr. Constable shows little emotion. He seems almost dour, except when he is with his wife, and then he becomes animated. After dinner they walk together. Long after bedtime, I hear them talking in the parlor. Sometimes they sound quite angry, but at other times they are laughing and happy. I have never known a middle-aged couple like these two.

Maggie, when you see Mama, you had better not mention any of this to her. She would worry about my living with so much casualness.

Your chum,
Lucy

December 23, 1911
At the Constable's

Dear Maggie,

I have not heard from George either, not in more than two months. What can he be thinking of, not answering your letters? Of course you cannot wait for him forever, but could you not wait just a little longer? Does he know you are going out with Bruce Weatherly? Oh, Maggie! I had planned on having you as another sister.

If you could have been with me at the Sully party, it would have been perfect. Remember the signal we used to have when during a party one of us would look across the room at the other and know whether she was having the time of her life. All evening I imagined you there, smiling at me, having fun.

The day of the party, we—Christobel, Amy, Amanda, and I—began dressing at three. The men, planning to come later because of a cow in trouble calving and a fence found down that morning, were out of the house, and we drew our own bath water and heated up the stove for the pressing irons. Christobel basted the ivory lace collar on my dress ("I can do this quicker than you," she said), and I did up her black hair, streaked with gray, in a thick, shining coronet of braids.

Bob came for me at five, and when we drove up to the ranch house, it was already ablaze with light. The stained-glass windows on the third floor caught the rays of the sun, already fallen below the horizon, and sent out swaths of green, purple and amber light to arriving guests. The front porch and the long stairway in the main hall were garlanded with pine (How forlorn my little tumbleweed tree seemed then!), shipped out from East Texas, and red velvet ribbons.

Mr. and Mrs. Sully and their two daughters, Carolyn and Lucia, received their guests at the foot of the stairs. Mr. Sully took my hand warmly in both of his, and Mrs. Sully leaned forward, offering her cheek. "Bob, you'll stay here and welcome our guests, won't you? Miss Richards has friends she can join," she said, dismissing me.

But most of the people there were strangers to me. Until the Constables arrived, I stood by the hall tree, already filled with hats—two of them clearly belonging to Yankees—watching Bob's sisters, not pretty as the Constable girls are pretty but, despite their Eastern educations, possessing an air of expansiveness. I liked them at once.

Then the Constable women arrived. Christobel wore a silk of forest green with pearls that gleamed against her olive skin, as dark as that of any of her sons, and she was, not beautiful—she's not a beautiful woman—but alive and warm. Amy and Amanda, wearing dresses of pale coral and peach, looked like tea roses from Aunt Catherine's garden.

And then, Maggie, I saw the strangest thing. Over quickly. Imagined perhaps? Mr. Sully moved as if to take Christobel's shoulders in his hands but then, without a word, dropped his hands to his side. Later, I joined him before the fire in the library and began to tell him about the tumbleweed tree and the students' excitement over it. Suddenly I realized he was not listening to a word I was saying. Deer hunters must wait as he was waiting, alert only to a sound not yet heard, a quarry not yet sighted. When Christobel came into the room, he moved from my side to hers without a word, and neither of them knew when I left the room.

As I crossed the hall I saw that Josh Arnold was in the parlor, standing in front of its white marble fireplace and talking with two men I had not seen before. Their more distanced manner said clearly these were the men to whom the narrow-brimmed hats belonged. When I entered the room, I heard Josh saying, "Hell, yes, there's hostility toward the railroad, and there's reason enough for it." Seeing me, he moved toward me and introduced Mr. Carrington and Mr. Albright: "These gentlemen are from New York. They're with the railroad." But before I had exchanged more than a few words with them, Bob came looking for me, and we went into the dining room to be served.

Maggie, remember how we used to dress up on Sunday afternoons in case a beau should come calling? And how flat it all went if no one did?

The Sully party was like that—beautiful, but it all went flat. The women, most of them ranchers' wives, gleamed like fine, old paintings in their Christmas finery, but there were no spontaneous sounds—the sudden bursts of laughter from a room, the quickened rhythms of guests moving from one place to another—sounds of people having a good time. It was as if we were waiting there for something that never happened.

The only flurry came when the Constable men rode in. When Cable saw Lucia, he picked her up off the floor and spun her around. Cable is *very* handsome and Lucia seems to know it. Mr. Albright and Mr. Carrington asked Josh who they were. He said, "That's the Constables. Ask *them* how they feel about the railroad."

Soon afterwards, Bob told me his mother needed him to see about their house guests. When he asked Christobel if I might ride home with her, I knew that for me the party was over.

Maggie, I had looked forward to it for weeks. Now it was over, and nothing was as I had imagined. Tonight, I feel very sad. If only you were here, we could cheer each other.

Your best chum,
Lucy

P.S. I think it was the presence of the railroad Yankees that put a damper on the party.

December 24, 1911
At the Constable's

Dear Lillian,

Tomorrow is Christmas. You and Edmund will be with Mama and Katie and Aunt Catherine. The crisp snow in the front yard, warmed by the sun from its winter angle, will have begun to melt around the edges, forming tiny freshets, narrow and glistening as the tinsel on the tree, but on the north side of the house, there the cedars will be, bowed low under still lavish mounds of snow, beatitudes of white and deep-down green. By now Aunt Catherine will have made the jam cake and the cornbread for the dressing; the stockings will be hanging, waiting to be filled with oranges and pecans.

And I am with strangers in a country more strange than any I could have imagined, but I will not feel sorry for myself. How can I when I think of the Christmas caroling at the school this morning?

The day before the party, Christobel had taken me down into the storm cellar, lined with shelves of okra, corn, tomatoes, and green beans, the jars gleaming like unpolished jewels in the dim light. At her insistence, I chose a jar for each of my students, including Carlos. "The Samses and the Wilkins, maybe the Baldridges, will not have had vegetables since last summer," she said. "Oh, maybe a little polk or dandelion greens, but not real vegetables."

Right after lunch the families began to arrive at the school. Mr. and Mrs. Baldridge with Baby Samuel, this time wearing a blue dress, came first. Mrs. Baldridge, her hair curling about her round, blue eyes, kittenlike, clean and sweet, looked shockingly different from her dirty, disheveled-looking children. Mr. Baldridge, apparently still somewhat angry because of the last school-board meeting, said, "I'll just wait outside until the rest of 'em come." When the Samses arrived, I understood why their children looked so much alike. The parents could be twins, and were it not for their clothes, it would be difficult to tell them apart. Mrs. Sams even has a slight moustache like her husband's.

Loretta Abernathy, Bucy's fifteen-year-old sister, came with her parents, and I discovered the most astonishing thing about her as she walked around the schoolroom looking at the tree and the children's work. "What's this?" she said, pointing to the word "Merry" written on a slate. Startled, I told her, and then I asked, pointing to the next word, "Do you know what this is?"

"Bet it's 'Christmas'," she said laughing. "I never been to school."

"She don't need it," her father said. "Her Ma never went."

I told Mr. Abernathy that in this day and age a girl needs an education as much as any man, and he said, "Loretta's Ma can't spare her." Mrs. Abernathy snapped, "It's *you* who has her in the field."

But Bucy's saying, "Jessie Sams can read better'n anybody in the room except me, and she's a girl," persuaded them both. Loretta will begin school right after Christmas, and Jessie Sams will have a friend her age to see every day.

Petey Constable, who has a natural talent for it, played the piano while the children sang the carols we had practiced. Then together we sang all the old, familiar ones, and as we sang, first the children, singing unabashedly, forgot themselves, and then the women's voices rose above theirs, and by the time we got to "Joy to the World," the singing of the men almost drowned the rest. Oh, Lillian, the wonder and the joy of a piano out here! It is the best present we could have had.

The party was almost over when I saw a lone woman walking across the prairie to the schoolhouse, and I knew it must be Berl Monday's mother, who, everybody says, is not quite right. To me, she seemed at once natural and strange. Dressed in black, her coat, her skirt, what might have been a veil, responded generously to the wind that blew first one way and then another so that one minute her body was outlined, a figure on the prow of a Viking ship, and the next, totally obscured. Then she seemed an apparition, swaying a dizzy path across the prairie.

Entering the room, she spoke to no one, not even to her son, but when he saw her he quickly covered his left ear with its missing ear lobe with his hand. (I've often wondered about that injury, such a savage one.) She sat with a kind of dumb patience throughout the program. Afterwards, I moved to speak to her, to take her hand, but I was interrupted by Mrs. Abernathy's profuse admiration of the tree: "It's the prettiest thing I ever seen," she said, and when I looked again, Mrs. Monday was gone.

I gave each a present, corn to Petey and okra to Squint from their own cellar so as not to make a difference, and as the students left, the younger ones gave me hugs and kisses, and the older ones, wide smiles and shy "Good-byes."

"Where do you think the piano came from?" asked Mr. Baldridge, who had stayed behind for just this question.

"I don't know. From Santa Claus, maybe."

At this response, his angry look said better than words that Mr. Sully might as well have left his card on it.

"Miss Richards," he said sternly, "we all know where that piano came from. And another thing, whether you like it or not, every kid in this school has to have his head washed with lye soap, and the schoolroom has to be fumigated. Miz Constable will see to it right after Christmas." Satisfied that he had put his foot down, he left.

It's as Josh says. Things are easier when you know how to go about them. Had *I* suggested this solution, Mr. Baldridge would have resented it, but because Mr. Constable brought up the lice problem at the school board meeting, he is perfectly satisfied. All it needed was a word from Christobel to her husband. Lillian, if women served on school boards (and why shouldn't they?), they wouldn't have to work through their husbands to get things done.

Love,
Lucy

P.S. Mama said she had mailed a box of clothes, but I have not yet received them. I hope they come soon because of this bitter cold. Although the Constables are able to help a little with food (Christobel sent over tins of tomatoes last week), nobody has clothes to give away.

December 25, 1911
At the Constable's

Dear Diary,

Christmas day for me. Such a day! This morning I "moped around" as Mama would say, missing my family and feeling gloomy because Bob had not asked me to spend Christmas with him.

The middle of the morning, I wandered out to the screened-in back porch where Christobel was tending a small, gray fox that Petey had found trapped, its fur matted and bloody, its leg almost severed. When he brought the poor creature in, it was in shock, but Christobel stopped the bleeding at once with a spider web dipped in lamp black. Now it lay in a cage, breathing hard, as if running the longest race.

"Lucy, heat a pan of water and bring it out here," she said. "I want to bathe this leg with carbolic acid water while the poor thing's unconscious."

While I waited for the water to heat, she fed both her red-tailed hawk, recovering from a bullet wound, and her mockingbird.

I brought the water out and watched as she bathed the ugly wound. "Lucy, look at this leg. I'm not sure we can save it," she said, washing it tenderly. Watching her, I was calmed by the ease and the sureness with which she worked. Her long black hair, swinging forward, hid her eyes, making more singular the fullness of her mouth, its generous upward curve more pronounced.

Feeling easier with Christobel than with anyone else, even Maggie, I said, "Bob sent a note saying he would drive over this afternoon, but he didn't invite me over for Christmas dinner with his family. I don't know why."

Christobel closed the cage door and stood up. "Lucy," she said, thoughtfully, "be careful what you want. Be careful. Sometimes a young girl, and you're that, does not always know."

"I may not be sure about what I want," I said, "but I am sure about what I don't want. These people out here have nothing. To live day in and day out like Mrs. Dawson, looking at her drab walls, her drab husband. I couldn't stand it!"

"I wouldn't want you to. Just wait awhile. That's all. Meantime," she said, cupping my chin in her hand, "I'll make you a cup of violet tea," and she smiled. "It will cheer you up in a minute."

When Bob came, he cheered me up more than the violet tea, more than talking to Christobel. "Close your eyes," he said, and he fastened a string of pearls around my neck. "When Mama gets over Dickie, we can be engaged. Wear these now and on our wedding day."

I put my arms around him and lifted my lips to his, enjoying the warmth of his chest against my breasts.

Christobel knows a lot, but she is wrong about this. I know what I want. I want to marry Bob Sully and live happily ever after.

Diary, do you suppose the Sullys will build us a weaning house on the ranch like the one the Constables built for Susan and her new husband?

Lucy

December 26, 1911
At the Constable's

Dearest Aunt Catherine,

Although it was a bitterly cold day, we have all been sterilized and fumigated. Christobel came to the school, and we started early to be sure the students' hair could get good and dry before school was out. We closed the windows and the door, and she started the sulphur burning. Then we all hurried to Mrs. Dawson's, for she had promised Christobel the use of her warm kitchen.

It was a two-part treatment. First, Christobel dabbed each head with cotton soaked in coal oil. Then she washed each with lye soap. Because every student was treated, it was accepted by all with good grace. I noticed, however, that when Christobel got to the Baldridges and the Samses, she was especially thorough.

When we went into the Dawson's house, I was as surprised as I had been that first time. Now it was as if anybody in Bonham might have lived there. Mrs. Dawson had made curtains for every window in the house, and there was a rocking chair in the kitchen and a rag rug on the floor in front of it. She had even baked Christobel's spice cake and had a pot of real coffee on the stove for us.

For a few minutes I felt happily responsible for it all. Then I noticed the slight swell beneath her apron and knew this richness came from a far more significant source than I. As Christobel treated each student's hair, enjoying the process, making a game out of it, Mabel Dawson said shyly, "It's been right lonesome since you left, but with a baby about we won't even hear the wind. We're real glad."

Aunt Catherine, I understand so well what she meant. I could never live alone in West Texas.

The school year is more than halfway over. Soon I'll be on my way home. I want to help Mama with the hardware business and help Lillian get ready for her baby. I want to sit down and tell you all about Bob—this, most of all.

Love,
Lucy

December 29, 1911
At the Constable's

Dear Diary,

Petey Constable has run away, and I know why. I must think what to do. I must tell someone what happened.

It was night before last, a cold, moonlit night. I heard a window being raised, followed by the sound of someone jumping lightly to the ground, and I knew it must be either Petey or Squint. I went to my window and plain as day saw Petey walking across the field toward the canyon bridge. I started to call out, "Petey, come back here this minute," but knew I'd wake the house, so I put on my shoes and bundled up in my cloak. I'll catch up with him, I thought. I will bring him home and tell him he needs to spend more time on math and less time at the piano. As I reached the barbed-wire fence, he disappeared, going down into the canyon. I stepped on the bottom wire and pulled up the top one to slip between the two, but I released them too quickly and heard my cloak tear and felt a sharp barb rake across my back. With the cold and the pain, I almost turned back.

I wish I had.

I watched Petey make his way down the canyon, and saw him going around the curve in the canyon wall toward the bridge. The urgency of his walk, its secretiveness, stilled the cry I might have made.

Oh, Petey, I thought. Where *are* you going? Holding on to the scrub oak, the shaker root, whatever offered a handhold, I found a way down, and following the curving canyon wall, I saw the bridge and knew it was as far as I needed to go. Petey was there. He had my silk shawl in his hands. As I watched from behind a clump of horsemint, he swung the shawl around his frail, thin shoulders, bringing the smoothness of the silk up to his cheek (How often I had made the gesture), and then, moving as if to some imagined music, he began to dance. Oh, here was a dancer! His *jetes* and *entrechats*, not learned (how could they have been?), as fine and strong as any ballerino's. When it was over, I could hear his breathing, slicing like a silver knife across the cold canyon air. I moved to tell him—what? To say his dance was beautiful, I think, and it's all, oh, Petey, it's all right about my shawl. He saw me and froze there. I stepped into the pool of moonlight where he stood and, like a frightened deer, he bounded away, leaving the shawl, a rush of white, a silver rivulet in the dry canyon bed.

He's been gone two days now. Oh, Petey, who cares about a shawl! If you'll just come home, this house can breathe again.

Lucy

December 31, 1911
At the Constable's

Dear Diary,

Josh was the first one sent for. He came to the school and questioned every child, asking over and over, "Where do you think Petey might be," and, "Did Petey ever say he'd like to go some place special?" It was Jessie Sams, looking out the window as if conjuring up the place, who said Berl and Bucy had called Petey a sissy. "He said he was going to Memphis or Paris," she said dreamily.

"France?" Josh asked, a little wildly. "Paris, France? Memphis, Texas?"

Jessie shrugged her shoulders. Josh and Mr. Constable left for Memphis this afternoon. Christobel, her live, green eyes, wounded and dazed, walked up and down the canyon, calling "Petey," "Petey," "Petey." We all looked, but out here there are not many places a boy can hide.

Lucy

January 2, 1912
At the Constable's

Dear Bob,

It is a quiet comfort to know that you and all the ranch hands are looking for Petey. At night his mother is in agony, realizing he might be cold or hungry.

He is so like her in his love of wild animals and his passionate response to beauty. I had not realized this until he ran away.

But it is hard to be different. Ever since the piano came, he has lost interest in recess, begging to be allowed to stay inside and play. The sight of his slender frame bent over the instrument, his long fingers spread over the keys, his total engagement with the piano, caused me to allow him more than once to stay inside. He has been set apart because of it.

Your,
Lucy

January 4, 1912
At the Constable's

Dear Diary,

On the day Mr. Constable and Josh went to Memphis, Mr. Sully came over to comfort Christobel. Petey's brothers and sisters were scattered all over the county looking for him, except for Squint, who had driven me home, and he was at the barn unhitching the wagon. I walked into the parlor, and Christobel was in Mr. Sully's arms, sobbing like a child.

"Chrissy, we'll find him. I promise we will. If I have

to tear up this whole county, we'll find him. Chrissy. Chrissy."

If they noticed me as I walked down the hall to my room, they gave no sign of it.

He loves her. I've known it since the night of the party at the ranchhouse.

I wonder how he came to that. I wonder where Petey is right this minute. I wonder about Berl Monday's mother.

And I wonder about something else. With the land so wide and flat, the stars so close at night, so *familiar*, how is it that this country is so filled with mystery?

Lucy

January 6, 1912
At the Constable's

Dear Josh,

It's hard to believe that after three days in Memphis, you and Mr. Constable found no trace of Petey. It was a relief to tell you about the night he ran away. I believe you are right. I will not burden Christobel with this. When Petey comes home, there will be time enough to think how best to help him.

Although this house is filled with comfortable things, there is not much beauty in it. Most likely, Petey took the shawl without thinking, in the same manner I would pick a bluebonnet from an East Texas field of wild flowers. But why did you tell me to lock my trunk?

Christobel walks along the rim of the canyon every evening, and Mr. Constable paces back and forth on the front porch, each in his own way looking for Petey. And each night Christobel goes to the canyon bridge (Do you suppose she somehow *knows* what happened there that night?) and hangs a pail filled with food from a railing, just in case Petey should come close.

Sincerely,
L. E. R.

January 6, 1912
At the Constable's

Dear Mama,

Petey Constable has run away from home. The hardest thing in this world is to wait for someone who does not come.

Through all of this I've thought about you. Not knowing where Katie is or when she's coming home! But don't you worry. I have a plan.

I am supposed to move to the Baldridges' in February, but what with their lice and Mr. Baldridge's temper, I just can't do it. I won't.

I am going to ask the trustees to build me a teacherage; rather, I am going to ask Christobel to take it up with her husband. Then Katie can come out here and live with me. Oh, Mama, building it would be the easiest thing in the world for the men to do. Fastened on to the school, only three outside walls would be needed, and inside there would be a bedroom, a small place to sit, and a tiny kitchen. I could paint the house myself and find furniture for it. Everybody needs a house, and, with Carlos sleeping in the school and H.H. by my bed, Katie and I would be as safe and cozy as rabbits in a nest.

Don't say a word to Katie about it yet. I want it to be a surprise. As soon as I talk to Christobel, (and I don't know when that will be), I'll write her. Christobel is heartbroken about Petey. We all are.

And dearest Mama, Edmund is right. You must insist that your customers pay their bills. How can Mrs. Weatherly look you in the face on Sunday morning knowing she owes you over ten dollars? The next time she comes in to buy as much as a feather duster, tell her she has no more credit in your store. Then the word will spread that Carrie Belle Richards is not a woman to be trifled with.

Love,
Lucy

January 11, 1912
At the Constable's

Diary,

Still no word from Petey. Last night I thought he had come home. We all did.

Right after I heard the train's whistle that signals the beginning of its ascent up the incline on the farm, H.H. began to growl. "Hush," I said, thinking one of the Constables was returning after opening and closing the gate for the train, but he kept on growling. Just as his growls changed to ferocious barking, there were footsteps on the front porch, followed by a loud knocking.

I put on my robe and went out into the hall. Amy and Amanda, blinking against the light from the lamp I carried, looking frightened, came out of their room, and Squint, snapping up his pants, came down the hall. Mr. Constable appeared a minute later, fully dressed, just as Christobel, in a robe, barefoot, came from the parlor where she had gone to get another lamp.

So we were all there in the hall, scared, expectant, breathless with hope, when Mr. Constable opened the door to the railroad men, Mr. Albright and Mr. Carrington who had been at the Sully's Christmas party.

"Sorry to wake you people this hour of the night, but when we got to Estelline we decided to ride the train on out here. When the train slowed down goin' up the hill on your place, we just hopped off. Ed here took a spill," Mr. Albright said.

"Jim, ask them to come in," said Christobel, adjusting the wick of a lamp she placed on the table in the hall. Now we could see his dark pants, torn up the side and streaked with red dirt.

Mr. Constable said, "What's your business out here? You come about Petey?"

"We're on railroad business. Doing a little investigative work," said Mr. Carrington. "Who's Petey?"

"Our boy. He's been gone ten days."

"Sorry to hear that. You think he jumped the train? It would be real easy the way it slows going across your farm."

"No. The train comes through here on Tuesday and Saturday, and he took off on Wednesday." Turning away, Mr. Constable said, "Investigative work, huh? You detectives? Well, I've got no use for the railroad, but that can wait 'til morning. You can bunk down here in the parlor. Squint, get some quilts."

As we moved to return to our rooms, we were stayed by other footsteps coming up on the porch, footsteps that set H.H.'s tail to wagging. The door opened and Cable stood there, his usually smiling face startled and solemn. "Dad, two men from the . . . ," and seeing them, he stopped.

"They don't know anything about Petey, Cable. They're doing some detective work for the railroad."

"Investigating what?" Cable asked, and his smile was back.

"Cable, we'll discuss it tomorrow. Now we're all going to bed."

Squint, putting his hand on his father's arm, said, "Dad, I'll sleep at the bunkhouse tonight. They can have my room."

Mr. Constable nodded, and we went to bed. I went right to sleep. When Squint and I left for school the next morning, Mr. Constable and the railroad men were in an earnest huddle, Mr. Albright and Mr. Carrington doing all the talking while Mr. Constable whittled, whittled away at another piece of wood.

When I walked out to climb into the wagon, I overheard Mr. Albright saying, ". . . and over a dozen cases of tomatoes, stolen."

They were gone when I got home, and I forgot all about them, for Petey has come back!

Joyfully,
Lucy

January 12, 1912
At the Constable's

Dear Diary,

Josh brought Petey home this afternoon. When we heard his car honking all the way across the canyon bridge, we knew he was bringing good news.

By the time Cable had run to open the gate and Josh had driven into the yard, we were all there. "Petey, where you been, boy? We've been worried about you," his father said, snatching the car door open, grabbing his son up, hugging him.

"Questions can wait, Jim," Christobel said. "He's worn-out. Look at him. Girls, go fix him something to eat. First, bring him some hot tea." She looked at Josh. "Thank God you found him."

But it was the other way round. "I went to Childress," Petey said. "Jumped the train on Saturday, rode it to Childress, and tried to find a job." He sat on his bed, looking down at his hands. His family hovered over him, Amy and Amanda not yet able to leave his side. I sat on the window sill behind him, afraid that if his eyes met mine, he'd again take flight.

"What did you do in Childress?" Squint asked, doubling up his fist, hitting him gently on his arm.

"One day I worked for two aeronauts. Hey, they went up in a basket under a balloon." He sounded excited, for a minute, and happy. "They fed me, but they didn't pay me nothin'. Tuesday I rode the train back to Estelline and found Mr. Arnold."

Josh put his hand on Petey's shoulder and said, "Jim and Christobel, Petey and I have had a good visit this morning. I want to talk to you, and this boy wants to talk to his teacher." He gave Petey's shoulder a squeeze and walked over to the door. "Could we do that while his sisters fix him something to eat?"

The girls and his mother hugged and kissed him, said they were glad to have him home, and I sat still, wondering what to say to Petey, what he might say to me. He has his mother's nature, I thought, looking at his narrow shoulders, his small head, but he doesn't look a thing like her. Christobel is tall and walks with long, determined strides. All the Constables do, and they're all olive-skinned with dark hair, except for Petey. The sudden movement of his shoulders as if to brush away the intrusion of my gaze made me say his name and then, "I'm glad you're home too, Petey."

He waited, his body tense, listening.

"Petey, I liked your dance. Once some dancers came to Dallas, and one of them danced just like you. A Russian. Strong leaps into the air. You must have practiced those a lot."

He straightened his back. I leaned forward, "Petey, who cares about a shawl."

"It was better before you came," he said angrily. He twisted around to look at me, his face flushed. "Nobody called me a sissy then!"

"Well, you're no sissy now. Who else would hop a train, get a job in Childress? Would Berl do that? Would Bucy?"

He put his hands on the bed, leaning on his left one, relenting a little.

"You made the schoolhouse nice," he said. "The leaves and berries. The piano. A Christmas tree. I liked that tree."

"I did, too, Petey. Everybody did."

"I was gonna put your shawl back. Your purse too."

"I knew that, Petey. I always knew my shawl would come dancing back." Encouraged by the quick, little smile I saw cross his face, I moved to the bed and sat down by him.

"Mr. Arnold and I have a plan," he said, and he took a long, deep breath and yawned. "He's telling Christobel and Daddy about it right now. It's a right good plan."

"That's the ticket," I said. "I'd like to hear about your plan."

The violet-colored circles under his eyes were large and symmetrical, evidence of his days of bruised wandering. Even his lips seemed faintly purple. I said, "Petey, I'm going to see about that tea right now. And some food. Then we can talk some more."

But when Christobel and I came with the hot tea and the vegetable soup, he was sound asleep.

The plan is that Christobel will take Petey to her sister in Boston. There he can study music and art along with reading, writing, and arithmetic. In the Boston Conservatory of Fine Arts, a young boy who plays the piano with such passion and dances with strength and grace will not be set apart. Mr. Constable has reluctantly agreed to the plan because Josh thinks it's a good idea.

Relieved,
Lucy

January 14, 1912
At the Constable's

Dear Katie,

I have a wonderful surprise. You are coming to West Texas to live with me in our very own little house. At least, I hope you are. Please say you will come. The White Star community is going to build a house for just the two of us.

Katie, we will have such fun. We'll be invited for weekends with the Sullys and the Constables. Cable Constable is just about the handsomest man, besides Bob of course, in Hall County. And Josh Arnold will take you everywhere in his motor car. He's much too old for you, but you will like him. Everybody does.

I asked Christobel about the teacherage this morning. At first she was doubtful about it, but I told her I was so homesick, I'd die if I couldn't have my sister with me for a while. And she certainly doesn't want me living with the Baldridges where I'd have to stay next. She went right to her husband, and he said, "No reason why not." Just think of it, Katie. He said, "No reason why not." How easy he made it all sound. Such a wonderful thing, sounding so easy.

I'm waiting for your answer. Please write me a letter right back. Write me and say, "No reason why not!"

Love,
Lucy

January 15, 1912
At the Constable's

Dear Mrs. Sully,

I accept with pleasure your kind invitation to spend the weekend at the ranch.

Your plans for a visit to the cemetery followed by an afternoon drive in your new closed-in buggy sound nice. I agree that driving about at a slower pace than a car travels has much to offer.

Sincerely,
Lucy E. Richards

January 17, 1912
At the Constable's

Dear Maggie,

Once again I am invited to the Sully ranch. I deliberately force my thoughts away from that last sad visit to the prospects of a far happier one next weekend.

I wonder if I will have my old room back. I wonder where Bob sleeps. Do you suppose his aunt and his mother will stand guard in the hallway between our two rooms? Maggie, the picture of them there, sitting back to back in their gowns and nightcaps tickles my funny bone.

We got Christobel and Petey off to Boston last night. Cable and Lacey walked westward along the tracks, each swinging a lantern, to signal the train we had passengers for it. Mr. Constable held firmly to his wife's arm as if he would never let her go, all the while saying, "Christobel, I'm glad you're going to see your sister. I'm real glad you two can have a nice visit."

Christobel, looking inordinately sad, hugged each of us as if she might never see us again. When the train was quite near, its whistle sounded, and H.H. sat back, gave a mournful howl, and took off across the pasture. Such a clown! Laughing at my silly dog, we ran alongside the train to the passenger car and helped Christobel and Petey on with their luggage.

"When you coming back?" Mr. Constable shouted as the train pulled away. But the whistle drowned out her reply. Remembering how I felt when I left all my family at the train station in Bonham, I cried a little for Petey.

With Christobel's leaving, all the music has gone out of the house. Everyone goes about the daily chores so quietly that now, even in the daytime, I can hear the easy *wisp, wisp, wisp* of the windmill. I hope I always have a windmill just outside my window.

Your chum,
Lucy

January 19, 1912
At the Constable's

Dear Diary,

I have my old room back at the Sully ranch. A cheerful fire fills the small pink marble fireplace, and my feet are warmed each night by a hot iron slipped between the sheets, linen sheets edged with lace and drawnwork and hemstitching a foot wide (I wish Aunt Catherine could see them), and, at bedtime, a smiling Alana brings me hot chocolate.

I was not surprised to learn that yesterday, just after Christobel left, Mr. Sully had also left, had gone up East. "Pa's gone to buy a railway car," Bob said when he came to get me at the Constable's. "He thought he had one in Jefferson, Jay Gould's old car, but now it's not for sale."

The Sully women were in the upstairs parlor when we arrived, Mrs. Sully in her husband's chair, her feet up on a stool, looked as if she had been housebound for a long time. Miss Grace Sully—tall, slender, unbending—rose and came forward, bringing with her the smell of lavender water, and embraced me gingerly. Mrs. Sully remained in her chair. "Hello, dear," she said, taking my hand in hers, smiling past me at Bob. "My son would like us to be better acquainted. I've planned a quiet weekend with that in mind. While he goes about doing whatever it is that he needs to do, you and Grace and I can have a nice, long visit."

"Ridin' fences, Mother. Tomorrow Shorty and I are ridin' fences all along the Constable farm."

Bob, one hand on my back, the other on my arm, walked with me to a loveseat, and when I was seated, stood behind it.

"Miss Richards," Mrs. Sully began, but I interrupted her.

"Oh, please, Mrs. Sully, won't you call me 'Lucy'? Miss Richards sounds so formal."

"Yes, of course, dear," she said. "Now, Lucy," and she pushed herself upright in her chair. (Was she now an invalid, I wondered. Had she been in an accident that had somehow gone unmentioned?) "Lucy, we were so glad that Constable boy came home. We were all worried about him."

Miss Grace Sully, sniffing as she spoke, nosing around her question, said, "Lucy, why in the world *did* the child run away? Do you know?"

"He is artistic and gifted and sensitive," I said, feeling my way carefully so as not to say too much. "The other boys don't understand him. I suppose he was lonely."

"Worrying his family to death! Having us all out looking for him! A boy like that needs a whipping," Mrs. Sully said, tapping the arm of her chair with her fingertips.

"That's not what he needs," I said indignantly. "He needs to be appreciated. He's fine and smart and musical."

Bob moved uneasily behind my chair, and I could have bitten off my tongue. Oh, Lucy, if you could just learn to be quiet *some* of the time, I thought to myself.

The next day Bob was off early, and his going eased the tension between his mother and me. We walked to the cemetery and stood, with Grace Sully, gazing down on Dickie's grave. Mrs. Sully took her handkerchief from her sleeve and dried the tears that ran down her cheek as I brushed off the marker, "Richard Lewis Sully/Beloved son: 1903–1911," with the hem of my skirt, but nothing could have persuaded me that that rectangular plot of dust had anything to do with the happy energy that had been Dickie.

Then we walked to the crest of the hill, and Mrs. Sully, looking westward, said with great satisfaction, "As far as you can see, Lucy, that land is ours. Did you ever see a prettier sight?"

The only disquieting note of the entire weekend came when, during our buggy ride, we saw Mrs. Monday on the road up ahead, her brown hair shining in thick braids across the top of her head and her clothes (were they black or brown?) swirling in a vortex of dust and wind and bright winter sunshine.

"That's Berl Monday's mother," I said. "I want to get to know her. Berl's in my classroom."

"Lucy, stay away from her," Mrs. Sully said, not unkindly. "Poor woman. She's just not right."

"Some say she's a witch," Grace said.

"I wouldn't repeat that nonsense, Grace. Why that's nothing but ignorant superstition," Mrs. Sully said sharply. "But I would stay away from her, though some say the men don't seem able to."

As we drew even with Mrs. Monday, she stopped, turned, and, shading her eyes, peered directly into the buggy. Greedily, desperately, her gaze sought mine, and I felt the shock one experiences from an unexpected blow, however light, or the sensation one feels when one is engulfed, briefly, by a whirlwind.

As we passed her, the two women leaned back in the buggy, but I, belatedly, stuck my head out and waved. "Hello, Mrs. Monday," I called back to her as she stood all alone in the middle of the wagon road.

It was not until I put my head on my pillow that night that I again saw Mrs. Monday's face and remembered the queer oddity of one brown eye and the other blue, and that blue one with a cast.

On Sunday after church, Brother Tinsley came to dinner. Although I do not find him handsome, Miss Grace Sully takes great pleasure in his company, and Bob great delight in teasing her about him.

The whole weekend was pleasant enough, but Bob and I were chaperoned so closely that we did not spend five minutes alone together until he drove me home in his automobile. Then I put my head on his shoulder and was asleep before we reached the Constable farm.

Lucy

January 21, 1912
At the Constable's

Dear Diary,

Last night H.H. did not come home for supper, and it was much too cold to leave my window open so he could come plunging through as he sometimes does. In the night I heard him whining to be let in. I opened the window and he jumped through it, still whining, but now with ecstasy as if *I* had been the one to leave *him*.

Suddenly thirsty, I put on my robe and hurried into the kitchen to get a drink of water. My attention was caught immediately by daytime sounds—a wagon creaking, Cable's voice, his words indecipherable, followed by Jonathan's, and then the sounds of the cellar's door being lifted from its slanting position, swung back, and then dropped—a series of sounds that is unmistakable. This was followed by the thump of boxes or cases being loaded onto the wagon.

Too sleepy and cold to care what the men were doing, I

hurried back to bed. The next morning I was mildly surprised to find only Squint and Mr. Constable at the breakfast table.

I think Christobel should come home. She has been gone far too long. It's as if she holds her husband's world in the palm of her hands, and she needs to bring it back. And her children, even the older ones, seem off-balance without her.

Lucy

January 22, 1912
At the Constable's

Dearest Lillian,

Your wonderful news came today, and I am happy for you and Edmund. Christobel says there's nothing in this world sweeter than a baby. With the extra precautions that Dr. Davis has advised, I am sure everything will go smooth as silk, and next September we will have a precious baby in the family.

When I come home for the summer, what fun we'll have getting everything ready. Let's paint the nursery yellow! I'm crazy about that color.

I had still another happy surprise today. Last week Bob said, "Lucy, you need a better way to get about than in the Constable wagon," but I had no idea he was planning to provide this better way. Today he came riding over with the prettiest little chestnut gelding I've ever seen. Gambol (Isn't that a terrific name?) is eight years old, very gentle, and has nice long sloping pasterns and well-laid-back shoulders that make him, according to Bob, the smoothest riding little horse in West Texas.

I have just had my first riding lesson under Bob's expert tutelage. I learned to saddle Gambol properly and to keep control as I mounted. Until I am confident enough to ride him to school, Bob says we will have a lesson every afternoon.

Gambol's only fault is that he shies at puddles of water, but in West Texas that will not be much of a problem.

Love,
Lucy

January 23, 1912
At the Constable's

Dear Diary,

Mr. Carrington and Mr. Albright returned today. Home alone, uneasy at the sound of a strange car coming into the yard, I waited, momentarily expecting a knock at the front door. When I did not hear one, I went to the front parlor and looked out the window. The railroad men were there, and, apparently thinking no one was at home, they had walked over to the storm cellar. I opened the front door and called to them, and Mr. Albright immediately walked back to the front porch. Mr. Carrington, as if reluctant to leave the storm cellar, followed more slowly.

"Everybody's in the field but me," I said. "Even the girls are working today, and Squint has just gone out. But come in out of the cold."

"Maybe you could help us, Miss Richards," Mr. Albright said. "I'm sure Mr. Constable's told you that somebody's stealing from the railroad. And we aim to find out who. Now, you teach here, you know these people, you know the Constables. Will you help us?" As he spoke, his eyes, filled with insatiable curiosity, never once meeting mine, darted over the horsehair chairs, the round table by the window with its oil lamp and clutter of *McClure's* and *Everybody's* magazines.

"*Can* you help us?" Mr. Carrington asked, his Adam's apple going up and down with each word. "Can you tell us anything?"

Startled, I shook my head.

Mr. Albright abruptly put down the magazine he had just picked up. "Some people out here don't like the railroad. The Constables, for one," he said.

"A lot of people don't like the railroad," I said. "Josh says the railroads need to be better regulated. He says that with three Texans in President Wilson's cabinet, Easterners won't be calling all the shots."

"What else does Mr. Arnold say about the railroad?" Mr. Carrington asked.

"Ask *him*," I said, disliking their prying questions and prying eyes, and thinking that neither ever *wears* a hat. "Why don't you just ask him?"

"Miss Richards, we're talking about stealing," Mr. Carrington said. "At first it was food, lots of it. Hams and cases of tomatoes and potatoes and sardines and beans. Then just before Christmas, an entire boxcar of furniture that was being shipped to the west coast was stolen."

"But couldn't that have been stolen anywhere between wherever the furniture was coming from . . ."

"Atlanta," Mr. Albright said. His eyebrows and eyelashes are the exact color as the pale red of his hair, his features nondescript until he smiles, and then his upper lip protrudes over his lower in a sharp point, a hornet's smile.

"Miss Richards, if anything occurs to you, just get in

touch with us. We're headquartering at the Sully ranch, and we will be there until we find the thief."

"Or thieves," Mr. Carrington added, almost lightly.

When I repeated the conversation at the supper table that evening, Jonathan and Lacey went right on eating. Cable looked at me and grinned. "If that's the case, they might be visiting the Sullys a mighty long time," he said.

I will not sleep a wink tonight. I do not want to believe what I know to be the truth. The Constables steal from the railroad.

It all falls into place. The presents Christobel wishes for and gets. Josh's warning to lock my trunk. The bountiful store of food, always on hand, with which they feed the hungry in the White Star community. The railroad men here asking so many questions.

And our piano! Could the piano be part of the stolen furniture shipment?

I don't know what to do about it, but this whole thing is about to break my heart.

Lucy

January 24, 1912
At the Constable's

Dear Christobel,

Come home as soon as possible. Mr. Constable is lost without you. Amy and Amanda go about their chores too quietly, and the customary roughhousing among the boys is absent. Even your mockingbird no longer sings.

Affectionately,
Lucy

JANE ROBERTS WOOD

Dear, dear Maggie,

I am surprised George has not answered your letters. Neither Mama nor I have heard from him, but I thought he would surely keep in touch with you. When I come home this summer, if you are still interested, the two of us can take the train to Tulsa and surprise him. Think about it. I am determined to have you in the family and, at times, a girl must take her destiny in her own hands.

Even as I write this next news I can see that little smile of yours, but out here men and women can be friends. Josh and I have become great pals.

Saturday he stopped by just as I was saddling Gambol for a morning ride. "Lucinda, mind if I join you?" he called, and almost before I could say, "Come ahead," he had asked Cable for the use of his horse, and had saddled Big Jack. You can judge his horsemanship when I tell you that I am a better rider than he is. Bob is a superb rider; even the Constables grudgingly admit he is the best in Hall county. Josh is a clown on a horse, bouncing all over its back, holding on to the saddle-horn, laughing at himself between his "gol-darn's" and "whoa now's" whenever Big Jack moved into a trot. But after we had crossed the canyon bridge, both horses settled some, and by the time we were past the schoolhouse, I was able to stop laughing at him.

Josh puzzles over this country. He says part of the problem between the farmers and the ranchers is that all through the ages any man on a horse has considered himself superior to a man who walked. That day the dust devils were blowing and there was a red cast in the sky that said there was a sandstorm coming. This caused Josh to think about conservation, which he says is necessary for the state's future. He is tickled that Governor Colquitt is in. He stumped for him last summer because he's against prohibition and for labor. Josh says he will be the best governor Texas has had since Hogg. Josh does make me think about things I'd never before considered.

The dust devils were all around us, perhaps a dozen or more, and Big Jack shying at them, when we saw Mrs. Monday coming from nowhere and going nowhere that I could see.

"Everybody says she is not quite right," I said.

"I wonder what they mean by that," Josh said, and as he spoke Mrs. Monday veered toward us, her passage, as erratic as the dust devils, sending a delicious chill down my spine.

"Hello, Mrs. Monday," I called, when I knew she was close enough to hear me. "How are you today?"

She stood immediately in front of the horses and waited until we must either stop or ride around her.

"Berl's teacher," she said and I smiled at her, unsure whether to look at her brown eye or her blue one. Her voice was sly and urgent. "I knowed you would come to see me. You been good to Berl." She shifted her gaze to Josh. "And with a nice man. Both of you come!"

She turned and walked away swiftly, now and then looking over her shoulder to be sure we were following, urging us on, commanding us. We walked our horses for perhaps a half a mile until we reached her house. No wonder I hadn't seen it. A dugout carved into a prairie knoll. The spear grass growing from the dirt roof and the small openings for the door together with its narrow window made it invisible until we had dismounted. Not till then did we see the steps that led us down to the front door.

"Sit down," she said, gesturing first to the only chair in the room and then toward a bed. As I took the chair and Josh sat on the bed, she untied the voluminous black shawl from around her head and shoulders.

"Coffee? Well, it's just parched corn," she said apologetically. I assured her that I'd enjoy anything as long as it was hot.

She dipped water from a bucket into a kettle, put the kettle on the stove, and poked up the fire. In spite of the cold wind outside, the dugout was quite warm. My eyes were growing accustomed to the dim light so that I could see the dirt floor, as clean as a pin, a dark quilt of no identifiable pattern on the bed, a lamp, two iron pots, a pepper box, and a small chest on the floor at the foot of the bed. And in the corner by the stove, there was a narrow cot. Berl's, I thought. I could not identify the smell that permeated the dugout, a smell of freshly turned earth just before a spring rain, of swollen promises and certain waiting. Living there, all by herself most of the time, no wonder Mrs. Monday seems strange.

"Mrs. Monday," Josh said, "I've never seen a house any cleaner than this one. You could give the ladies in White Star a lesson in good housekeeping."

"Every Saturday Berl brings the water, and I clean the place," she said proudly, swinging her long, thick braid over her shoulder to fall below her waist.

She opened the tin chest and took from it a china teapot, two cups, a saucer and a sugar bowl. "From my friend," she said proudly.

"Mrs. Monday, these are beautiful," I said. "Why, I don't often have coffee from a china cup."

Mrs. Monday poured the strong, black drink into the eggshell-thin china and then, surprisingly, sat on the bed close to Josh, watching with great satisfaction as he drank. When she did not join us, I assumed we were drinking from her only teacups.

"Mrs. Monday, I am glad your son is in my school. I hope he can stay the whole year. He told me he had to quit early last year to chop cotton."

"This year my boy will stay," she said. "Things is good for us this year. Better'n last."

"Berl has never mentioned his father, Mrs. Monday. Is he . . ."

"Gone," she said, looking at Josh, smiling, "and out here a woman shorely needs a man."

Then, Maggie, the roof just fell in. A whiff of dust, a scrambling sound of hoofs directly overhead, the muffled sound of earth clods falling, and then a cow's hoof right through the roof! And we were covered with dirt! Now the cow was bawling, and Josh, followed by Mrs. Monday, was up and out of the dugout before I realized what had happened. Then I ran outside.

Josh had one hand on the lead rope, holding the cow's head, while with his other hand he was trying to pull the cow's leg from the hole in Mrs. Monday's roof. A calf, chased by Mrs. Monday, was running back and forth across the dugout roof. And I was laughing. Oh, Maggie. I couldn't help it! Such a scene! Twice as funny because of the startled look on Josh's face a few minutes earlier when Mrs. Monday had said, "Out here, a woman shorely needs a man."

When Josh and Berl (who had come running when he heard the commotion), finally got the cow off the roof, Josh walked close and growled, "Well, gol-dern it, Lucy. Just stand there and laugh!" Then he inspected the damage inside the house, and Berl and Josh together decided how the repairs could best be made. Josh hastily thanked Mrs. Monday for the coffee and said, "I don't know about Miss Richards, but I need to be riding back."

Of course I joined him, still laughing and trying not to, for Josh obviously saw nothing funny about it. I tried to control my laughter. I'd stop for a minute, but then I'd remember Mrs. Monday's saying she needed a man, and Josh's trying to get the cow unstuck while the calf and Mrs. Monday ran in circles, and then I'd get tickled again. Josh didn't say a word, but his back got stiffer and straighter. Then for no reason, I thought about Josh's riding ability, or lack of it, and that set me off again.

All of a sudden, "Whoa," said Josh, pulling up Big Jack. "So you think it was funny, do you?" he asked, and his voice was as grim as your daddy's is when a teller's short at the bank. "Well, it is funny," he said, and he threw back his head and laughed, and we both sat there out in the middle of nothing and laughed together.

"I wonder how she survives out here," I said when we were again headed toward home. "How does she get along? How does she manage?"

"Poor, desperate woman. It's pretty clear to me how she manages," Josh said.

So Maggie, Mrs. Monday *is* one of those! In Paris or Dallas, yes, but imagine, out here in West Texas—a woman who sells her favors!

Maggie, you would like Josh. Sometimes he laughs at people, while at the same time he's feeling sorry for them.

138

Bob has been at the Henrietta ranch in Wichita Falls this past week. He will be home on Saturday, and I have so much to tell him.

Love,
Lucy

P.S. The cow was one loaned by Mr. Sams to Mrs. Monday for the milking.

January 27, 1912
At the Constable's

Dear Diary,

As soon as Bob got home from the Henrietta ranch today, he drove as fast as his car would go, twenty-three miles an hour, to see me. School was just out, and the twins and Jinks Mayfield, whispering madly, were the last to leave. Bob, amused at being the object of so much attention, waited until they were out of sight. "Now, Lucinda," he said, and placing his hands on my shoulders, he kissed me more fervently than ever before. Then he gently brushed my lips again and again with his until I caught his face between my hands and returned his kisses ten-fold.

We sat on the steps while he told me his dad was going to sell off all the cattle on the Henrietta ranch and turn that spread into a sheep ranch. He said the cattle growers would resent it, but his father believes in change if change is necessary.

I started to tell him I thought that Cable and Jonathan, maybe Lacey, were stealing from the railroad, but when I mentioned their names, his contempt of them was so obvious that it seemed for me to accuse them would be to malign dear friends. And I thought of the railroad men, waiting at his ranch like vultures. Mr. Carrington's eyes are cold, and there is something about Mr. Albright I cannot abide. Mama has always said you can't trust a man who doesn't wear a hat and neither of them does. So I said nothing.

When Mr. Sully comes home, I will talk to him, or if I can find the courage, I will talk to Cable and Jonathan. Across from them at the breakfast table, I do not believe they are thieves. But late at night, I begin to wonder.

Lucy,

January 29, 1912
At the Constable's

George Richards!

Married since Christmas and not telling any of us. Why? Of course, Mama is hurt. So am I. So are we all. Every mother expects to attend her son's wedding. To be denied this pleasure (I believe it is a right), is to be callously shut out of an important part of a son's life.

I have been in correspondence with Maggie Owen, and I know, for she has said as much, she loved you. This news will be hard for her to bear. But now, it's over and done with. And, frankly, to know you are well and happy is the best news I have had in months. The snapshot you sent of Inez tells me much about the woman you married. I see a young woman, her hands on her hips, her chin thrust forward, smiling into the sun, and I know she must have both a strong will and an appetite for fun.

What kind of car is she standing in front of? I have never seen one so long. But then, I have not seen many.

Love,
Lucy

P.S. Writing to you has completely dispelled the anger I felt when I began this letter. I believe the anger rose in part from my unease when week after week passed and I had not heard from you. I love you and I will love Inez. I am glad you are taking her to see Mama soon.

January 30, 1912
At the Constable's

Dear Diary,

Christobel came home two nights ago, came in the Sullys' own railway car. Cable had gone to make sure the tracks were clear, so it was he who greeted his mother and carried her bags to the house. Calling to us all, "Wake up, everybody, I'm home," her voice sounded as sweet as ever.

That first day she found time to spend with each of her children. I had forgotten how tall she was until I saw her riding with Squint, leaning into his voice, her shoulders almost level with his. When Bob brought me home from church, Christobel and Cable were sitting in the front porch swing in the cold sunshine, Cable laughing, telling his mother about a practical joke he had played, and Christobel nodding, smiling with quiet pleasure at each word. Long after I had gone to bed that night, I woke up to hear her voice and her husband's coming from the parlor.

By Monday afternoon, the house had settled to a quiet hum, and Christobel and I went for a walk along the dry river canyon bed. When we came to the bridge, we sat on the lowest trestle, a place just beyond that where I had seen Petey dance so long ago.

"He sent you this," she said, taking from her pocket a

handkerchief, unrolling it, and from it delicately holding up a silver chain, as fine as a spider's web.

"It's beautiful," I said fastening the chain around my neck. "How is he? Everyone asks. Does he dance and study music?"

"And drawing and painting and sculpture," his mother said. "Petey's real happy, but he misses his father and his brothers and sisters. He misses you, too."

Christobel stood and walked to the canyon wall, in winter as dry and hard as granite. She's thin, I thought. That's why she seems taller. Her waist is as slender as mine.

Crossing her arms, leaning against the canyon wall, she poked at a rock with the toe of her shoe. "Lucy, I thought of leaving him," she said. "I wouldn't, after all, be leavin' the children. Pretty soon they'll be leaving me. But . . . oh, it's kind of silly," she chuckled, "I couldn't leave my garden or the animals. And Mrs. Dawson will be needing me this spring. I couldn't leave," and her gesture encompassed the whole of the canyon, the prairie, the sky, "this place."

She walked slowly on down the canyon, and she might have been talking to herself as I walked along beside her. "Since the railroad came," she said, "between Jim Constable and me there's a wall, and he's put that wall between me and the boys. All but Petey." She stopped and, gazing up at the railroad bridge, she said, "I dislike the railroad as much as Jim does. But for different reasons." Then she smiled that great, warm smile of hers and, linking her arm in mine, she said, "Now tell me all about Bob. Tell me about you and Bob. Lucy, it is so wonderful to be loved! I want to know everything."

And in her presence, time became a fine, green mist,

and in the magic of the telling, I forgot about the pain in her voice when she told me she had thought of leaving her husband.

Tonight her words, "It is so wonderful to be loved," ring in my ears, and I wonder if it was her husband or Mr. Sully that she meant.

Puzzled,
Lucy

February 2, 1912
At the Constable's

Dear Aunt Catherine,

It rained last night. Jim Constable was the first to know it was coming. After supper was over and the dishes done, Christobel, Mr. Constable, the girls, and I sat in the parlor, enjoying the warmth of the fire.

The dust, blown by the high winds, sifted into the house, acrid and dry. Mr. Constable walked out into the yard and stood, looking intently at the sky. "Rain's coming'," he said when he came back in, "before mornin'."

"How can you tell?" I asked, doubting the possibility.

"Watch the birds," he said. "They know it."

I put on my cape and ran outside. The birds were usually easy this time of day, the sparrows perched atop fence posts or in mesquite, contentedly twittering, and the larger birds—the mourning doves, grackles, an occasional hawk—making long, tranquil loops against the pewter-colored sky. But now as I watched, they, as if scattered by the sound of gunshot, were flying erratic patterns and calling excitedly to each other. Pretty soon afterward we saw the first streak of lightning, miles away. After the others had gone to bed, I sat in my window thinking about Bob, watching the white, jagged streaks slash the sky. I watched until I heard the distant rumble of thunder and caught the first sweet whiff of rain. Then I pulled back the curtains and opened my windows a crack. I lay awake until late in the night listening to the great sheets of water that swept across the roof. I woke up this morning, thinking, for just a minute, I was in my own bed in Bonham.

Gambol is so uneasy with water that we will lead him behind the wagon, and I'll ride to school with Squint. Then Squint can come home to help with the clearing, and I can stay to plan our work for tomorrow.

I know the students will be excited. The rains have made the prairie a world of shallow lakes and small streams and frogs everywhere! Where did they all come from?

Lucy

February 2, 1912
At the Constable's

Dear Diary,

I am in bed with a bandaged knee, bruised bones, and a sore spirit.

Neither the Baldridges nor the Samses came to school this morning, and with just six students present, we finished our work early and had a wonderfully long recess, walking around pools of water, some of them almost as wide across as a pond. At noon, we watched the swollen river move sullenly along.

The students had to get home to help with the clearing, and they left as soon as school was out. After I had marked papers and planned assignments for the next day, I told Carlos good-bye and saddled Gambol, happy at the idea of riding through the cold, crisp, sweet-smelling afternoon.

Trembling, tossing his head, snorting, Gambol put one foot down, and then the other, gingerly pawing the ground before each step. We carefully made our way around pools of water, and soon he had settled enough for me to enjoy the clean, rain-washed countryside.

Suddenly, something (it could only have been a frog), splashed into a pool of water almost under his nose, and he was running, out of control, running blindly through the puddles of water and along the ground.

For a mile or two, I tried to hold on. Then I realized I was about to slip off. To seat myself more firmly, I reached back to grasp the saddle for balance, and at that instant Gambol swerved. And I was on the ground.

I lay there, hearing his hoofbeats fading away and feeling H.H.'s tongue on the back of my leg. Cold, numb all over, except for a sharp stinging sensation in my knee, I sat up slowly and examined my wounds. My leg and both my hands were scraped raw, and from a cut in the center of my knee, a slow trickle of blood ran down my leg.

I stood up slowly and looked around. There was not a house, not a human being, not even an animal in sight, and I wasn't even sure of the direction in which Gambol had run. But I knew the Constable farm was west of the school and, limping painfully, I made my way in that direction. Stopping to rest after a few minutes, I saw off to my right, as if by magic, Mrs. Monday's roof; small

whorls of smoke were coming from the stovepipe stick-
ing through the center of the mound of spear grass.

Oh good, I thought. I can get warm and bandage my
knee here, and Berl can get word to the Constables.

"Mrs. Monday. Oh, Mrs. Monday," I called, certain she
was home, but when I hobbled to the door and knocked,
there was no answer. Knowing that in West Texas no one
ever locks a house, I pushed open the heavy door and
had stepped inside before I realized that there in her bed,
sitting up, his legs crossed, was Mr. Albright, a toad of a
man. "Oh," I said, "excuse me," and I turned and tried to
run, but not before I had clearly seen Mrs. Monday, nude,
hunkered down behind the door, her reddish brown braid
falling in sharp contrast to the black puff of hair between
her legs.

Not thinking at all, I limped away from the house, and
there was Berl, coming toward me. "Gambol ran away,"
I said.

"You're hurt," he said, looking at my torn, bloodied
dress, my scraped hands. "And you're cold. Come on.
Mama will help you."

"Oh no, Berl. That's all right," I said, glancing toward
the dugout. From that angle, I could see Mr. Albright's
car behind the small rise, glittering in the sun's evening
rays. Berl's eyes followed my line of sight.

"Why that . . . !" he gasped. "I told him to stay away
from Mama."

He threw down the hoe he was carrying and sprinted
toward the dugout. I watched him go inside and a minute
later saw Mr. Albright walk hurriedly to his car. I turned
away and, as I had known I would, soon heard the sound
of his car come alongside me and stop.

"Miss Richards, get in. I'll take you home," he said.

Knowing I couldn't walk all that way, I stepped up on the running board and sat down. "Thank you, Mr. Albright," I said coolly, sitting as far from him as possible, not saying another word.

"I *am* good to her, Miss Richards. Always giving her trinkets. And money." My silence seemed to heighten the whining note in his voice. "I'd marry her if I could," he said, and I thought of a calf, bawling for its mother. "She thinks her husband is still alive somewhere."

"What about your wife?" I asked.

"Well, there's that, too," he said, his hands tightening on the wheel of the car. "But that boy of hers. He threatened to kill me just now. She sure better do something with him," he finished lamely.

When we got to the gate I said, "This is far enough, Mr. Albright," and without thanking him, I opened the gate and walked up to the house.

Now I'm warm and resting, Gambol has found his way home, and my knee has almost stopped hurting.

I'm going to tell Bob all about this. He will not want to hear it, but our worlds will be close only if we share them.

Lucy

February 3, 1912
At the Constable's

Dear Maggie,

More than anything else I miss the band concerts, the musicals and the Bonham Playhouse theatricals. Do write and tell me what the newest fashions are. By the time I come home this summer, I will be so hopelessly out of style you'll not want to be seen in my company.

Yes, I am still in love with Bob, and he returns my

affections. When he is at the White Star ranch, we see each other once, sometimes twice a week. So that we might more fully share our separate worlds, I have just this week decided to tell Bob everything I experience. I feel that a complete openness will bring him and me closer together. Why does honesty between a man and a woman seem so impossible before marriage and so necessary after?

Maggie, I have so much to tell you, so many experiences to share. I am years older than when I left home last fall.

Your best chum,
Lucy

February 4, 1912
At the Constable's

Dearest Katie,

Today I read the sweetest, best words in the English language. "No reason why not!" Until that moment, I had not known how much I missed you and needed you. The tears that filled my eyes sprang from happiness. The thought of having my little sister with me colors my whole world with joy.

Take the train to Estelline any time after March 1st. The teacherage will be finished by then, and we can move right in.

Christobel is going to help me make curtains, and you and I can paint. Please ask Aunt Catherine to make a rag rug for the bedroom and one for the kitchen, too. And when you come, bring my goose-down comforter and plenty of quilts. The cold out here is not a damp cold, so it seems warmer than it really is until the wind blows. Then nothing can keep out the rawness of it.

I am counting the days until March. I can hardly wait.

Love,
Lucy

February 5, 1912
At the Constable's

Dear Diary,

Today a letter from Mama saying Aunt Catherine has pleurisy and that every breath she takes is like a knife in her chest. Best aunt in the world. The kindest. If Katie were not practically on her way out here right now, I would take the next train home.

I remember my last day at home. Leaving. That was all I thought about. That morning I feel it in my bones before conscious thought, before I open my eyes to the sun's first rays coming through the curtains at my window, making a design of swirling circles and wavy filaments on the oak floor. Leaving home. From the garden comes Aunt Catherine's voice —small, firm—a resonant reflection of her physical self. Her, "Uncle Jerry, these beans are 'bout ready for tying up," and "Better work in a little ash round the tomatoes today," are interspersed with Uncle Jerry's soft, "Yes, M'am, Miss Catherine," and, "Sho do seem like it," their sentences braiding a cocoon for me to fall back into sleep again. Waking, I pad downstairs, barefooted, across the living room rug, through the kitchen to the sink. I splash my neck, my shoulders, my face, reaching blindly for the towel that hangs below. Then I put on my wrapper and walk out back to the privy. Here, the smell of wood scrubbed down with boiling water and lye soap. The scavenger man must have cleaned it recently. I leave the door open a crack to see the Queen Anne's lace growing just outside. The clusters of small, white flowers float above the thick, green stems, seemingly unconnected to them, airy as mist in the cool morning air.

Dressed, I join the two in the garden. Aunt Catherine is picking beans, her fingers moving quickly on the beanstalks. Uncle Jerry, moving slowly and stiffly, decorously addresses the garden lettuce, "Now then, jes' let me have a few of these leaves now," and the tommacky cabbage, "If'en I can take just this one nice head now, for Miss Lucy."

"Uncle Jerry, why aren't you at the hardware store today?" I ask.

"Seems like Miss Catherine need me more here in the garden than your Ma does at the store, Miss Lucy. Gettin' ready for your last day here." His eyes are blood-rimmed; his hands old and gnarled as the bark of an oak.

"Lucy, you ever see such a . . . ," but the rest of Aunt Catherine's question is lost in a spasm of coughing.

"Now, Miss Catherine, you overdone yo'self. You best go and res' now. Let Uncle Jerry see to da garden."

In the front porch swing, Aunt Catherine and I snap beans.

"Seems like I just can't get rid of this cough," she says.

"You're thinner," I tell her, alarm rising from the center of my stomach, tightening my throat. "You've always been thin, but you're thinner now than you've ever been."

"I'll be all right, Lucy. Sometimes a summer cough is the hardest thing to shake."

It is almost noon when Katie wanders into the kitchen.

"Beans again. Ugh," she says softly. Everything about Katie is soft. Her long hair, the color of sweet corn; her hands, small and plump; her gray eyes, the color of a mourning dove, fringed by long gray lashes.

"Aunt Catherine had to go to bed," I tell her. "You'll have to help with the dinner."

"I'd like to Lucy, but I can't. I promised to walk downtown with Lady Jones."

From the bedroom comes Aunt Catherine's voice, joining mine as we parody Mama, "When you go past the barber shop, DON'T LOOK IN!" We laugh, the three of us, Aunt Catherine's laugh broken off by a spell of coughing.

Christobel is calling me to come to the table. I'll ask her what to do about pleurisy.

Worried,
Lucy

February 5, 1912
At the Constable's

Dearest Aunt Catherine,

By the time you receive this I know you will be better. Christobel says pleurisy can be cured by boiling the taproot of the butterfly weed, inhaling its steam and drinking the tea. Have you used this remedy? I imagine you have, but I do not want to neglect to mention something that might be of some benefit to you.

Please write soon and tell me you're well again.

Love,
Lucy

JANE ROBERTS WOOD

February 7, 1912
At the Constable's

Dearest Sweetheart,

You have just ridden off, and Surprise's hoofbeats as he trotted across the canyon bridge have faded away. But I still feel your lips on mine, your hands where hands never were before and your strong, lean body pressed against mine.

What a glorious day for us! Glorious in a way I had never known it could be. After we had eaten the fried chicken and the apricot pie and sat snuggled together in the blankets in your car, I looked into your blue eyes the color of the sky, and I knew that I had been born and had lived for just this moment. You felt it too. I know it.

When can we be together always? Although the wound caused by Dickie's death will heal, his family will always mourn him. To wait a whole year to announce our engagement seems excessive, but I will, of course, bow to your mother's wishes in this matter.

Lovingly yours,
Lucy

February 10, 1912
At the Constable's

Dear Diary,

The last three days I have been filled with the sheer joy of being alive.

When I arrived, I rode through a desolate country, but today it seems a land teeming with life and sound and color, more beautiful than any place I had ever imagined. I know this is because Bob is here, a part of it all.

He has been over every afternoon, staying later and

later each time he comes. We've ridden together and eaten together and danced together. We have been closer than ever before. Our hands, as if they have wills of their own, meet in prelude to hungry journeyings over each other's bodies. I love the feel of his firm shoulders and slender back beneath my hands as all the while his arms pull me closer and closer to him, but never close enough.

We must somehow find a way to be together. If not, we must stop seeing each other. I shudder at the thought of becoming another Mrs. Monday.

In love,
Lucy

February 11, 1912
At the Constable's

Dear Diary,

Last night Bob told me his parents were sending him to manage the Henrietta spread for the next few weeks. I see Mrs. Sully's hand in this. How I dislike that woman! I can imagine her waiting up for him every night and becoming more and more alarmed as he came home later and later. He said as much to me yesterday. Although he has just left, already I miss him. I must fill these empty days somehow. For one thing, I will teach my students more. Josh says the quest for knowledge is man's most exciting journey. Josh obviously doesn't know much about love. The two just cannot be compared. However, I think teaching is exciting. But to teach more, I must know more. I will ask Josh for the loan of some books, particularly Mr. John Keats' poems. Josh said Keats had written a poem that fits me. I want to read it. I am curious.

Lucy

February 11, 1912
At the Constable's

Dearest Sweetheart,

I miss you so much. I love you so much. My eyes hunger for the sight of your face, and I long to hold you in my arms.

Does this surprise you? It surprises me. I had thought that women did not feel as men do. I was wrong.

Yours,
Lucy

February 12, 1912
At the Constable's

Diary,

A man dead! A man who breathed and spoke and walked—dead! Hands above his head. No, not his head. Hands above the empty air. Where his head should have been, only small, white, bloodless cords spilling out beyond the blood, already gone dark, that filled the cavity of his neck.

I can write no more.

Lucy

February 13, 1912
At the Constable's

Dear Mr. Sully,

I have asked Carlos to deliver this note. I must see you immediately. The question I must ask is so urgent it will not keep. Please come as soon as possible.

Gratefully,
Lucy E. Richards

THE TRAIN TO ESTELLINE

Dear Josh,

I have just sent a note to Mr. Sully asking him to come to the school immediately. I am going to ask him if he is our benefactor. Only then will I know what to do about the piano. The murder makes this information crucial to me. Yes, it was murder. I *know* it. You were there. That night, you were there! What happened? *You must know.*

Sheriff Ponder is on his way out here, and I am going to tell him everything. About the piano. About Berl. Berl was not in school today, and Mrs. Monday sent this note:

Dere Mis. Rishurds,
     Berl ain't feelin gud. Cum see hem.

Gladys Monday

But you didn't know that Berl had threatened to kill him, did you? Just last week. And the Constables. Behind Cable's laugh and Jonathan's shyness, I saw the hate that flared when Mr. Carrington said they wanted to look around the farm.

Let me take ten deep breaths, and then I'll tell you everything that happened before you came that night.

That afternoon, late, Mr. Albright and Mr. Carrington came snooping around again. We were in the field when they came. Because the Constables wanted to get the land cleared before plowing time, we were there working steadily, all but Squint, who had gone into White Star for supplies. Even Susan and her husband were there, and after I got home from school, I had joined them. We were planning to work until dark, and Christobel and Amy had brought hot coffee to the field and then gone back to the house to start supper. Mr. Constable, who never stops long, had finished his coffee and had walked about fifty yards away to the place where he was clearing some mesquite when we heard the car. He never looked up, but Cable grinned and winked at Jonathan.

I watched Mr. Albright and Mr. Carrington as they got out of their car and came walking down to the field.

"You folks are really working," Mr. Carrington said.

"If your hand'll fit a hoe," Cable said, "I got one for you."

Mr. Albright, obviously embarrassed in my presence, looked only at the ground in front of him, but Mr. Carrington laughed once and then stood staring at us all.

"Wonder if you'd mind if we looked around your place a little?" he said, finally.

Lucy, I said to myself, tell them about the piano. Tell them that just before Christmas, a piano turned up on the school ground. I opened my mouth to speak but, "You'll have to ask Daddy about that," Cable said. "It's his place."

We watched as Mr. Constable, who still had not looked up, steadily chopped away at the mesquite. Finally, he stopped and stood a minute, gazing at us through the evening twilight. Then, still carrying the axe, he began to walk toward us.

"Evening, Mr. Constable," Mr. Carrington said, calling out to him.

"Yep," Mr. Constable said, never pausing in his stride.

"We'd like to look around your place," Mr. Carrington said. "Be all right?"

"What for?" Mr. Constable's knuckles, as he gripped the axe handle, were as white as a frog's belly.

"Railroad's lost over fifteen hundred dollars worth of shipping since November," said Mr. Carrington.

There was a long silence while Mr. Constable carefully

laid down his axe, took out his knife, opened it, and then, apparently finding nothing to whittle, closed and pocketed it again. "You accusin' anybody?" he asked mildly.

"No. No," Mr. Albright said, jumping in. "We're just doing our job."

"We could get a warrant," Mr. Carrington said, looking off into the setting sun.

"Go ahead and look," Mr. Constable said. "You boys look if you want to. Look all over the seven thousand acres. But be off my place tomorrow and don't come back with a paper either. After this, you want to look around, you bring the sheriff."

He picked up his axe and walked toward the house. He met Christobel coming out to the pump for water, but I don't think he said a word to her.

When Mr. Carrington and Mr. Albright walked up to their car, Christobel, who had no idea that in the last half-hour the two had become her husband's enemies, asked them to stay for supper. And astonished, perhaps, by the invitation, they accepted. They were at the table, we all were, when Mr. Constable came up from the barn. He never shows much emotion, but when he saw them there, his mouth fell open.

During the silent meal, only Mr. Carrington attempted conversation. His comments, "A rain just now would sure help you folks along" and "I believe this is the finest chocolate pie I ever tasted," might as well have been rocks chunked into the middle of the table for all the friendliness with which they were met. Mr. Albright left the table several times, and each time returned visibly more inebriated. The last time he knocked over his chair and sat down on the floor.

"Well, damn," he said.

Mr. Carrington jumped to his feet as if to help him up, but then he just stood there, glaring down at him.

"Aw now, Car. I ain't a gonna give nothin' away." A whining note was again in his voice, the one that had been there when he drove me home from Mrs. Monday's after my fall. Now Mr. Albright, attempting to put his finger to his lips in a gesture of silence, missed and instead rested it alongside his nose. "S-s-s-s-sh. It's your secret, Car, and I'll never . . . " But Mr. Carrington didn't wait for the rest. He grabbed the fallen man by his shirt collar and belt and half-carried, half-dragged him from the house. It was at least twenty minutes before he returned, red-faced and, even in the bitter cold, perspiring. "I got him in the car," he told us grimly, but Mr. Albright was not there when Mr. Carrington was ready to leave. And no one, I least of all, was interested in finding him. But I was and am interested in what Mr. Albright started to say. What secret of Carrington's did he almost tell?

Just when Mr. Carrington was driving away, you came. By that time Cable had ridden off to see, so he said, "the sweetest lips in Hall county," and Jonathan and Lacey had gone to look for Lacey's peg pony that had broken out of its stall and strayed.

As I drifted off to sleep that night, I heard you say, "That's a dirty. . . . " Then the wind picked up, and the rest of the words were lost.

I cannot write about the pitiful thing I discovered on my way home the next day except to say that the rope marks on the wrists were deep. The man's hands had been bound together. This I clearly saw. This is what I must tell Sheriff Ponder when he comes.

I am going to see Mrs. Monday tomorrow.

Lucy

THE TRAIN TO ESTELLINE

February 14, 1912
At the Constable's

Dear Josh,

Only Berl Monday was absent from school today. All my pupils had heard about poor Mr. Albright. Jinks Mayfield asked if the train had turned him inside out. Bucy Abernathy read aloud a brief account from the *Childress Daily News* that mentioned me and Sheriff Ponder. The Baldridge twins said Mrs. Monday had put a spell on Mr. Albright so he just lay down on the track and waited for the train to run over him. Oda Ray said that just the day before Mrs. Monday had made Mr. Sams' cow go dry.

I stopped the math lessons immediately and substituted a lesson in logic. I pointed out that most cows, falling through a roof, would go dry. Together we separated fact from superstition and vanquished the question of Mrs. Monday's witchery for all time.

After school I set out for Mrs. Monday's, again seeming to come upon her house as if by accident. Such a chill ran down my spine when I saw the tin stovepipe shining through the grass that I was not too sure all superstition was gone.

But the sight of the grieving woman who answered the door swept away any silly fears I had. "Berl's gone," she sobbed. "He said he was leaving. Said he'd jine up or git work." Crying weakly like a very old woman, she lay down on the bed, covering her face with her apron.

Now it was I who made the parched corn coffee and got the teacups out of the chest. While the water heated, I ran outside, untied my lunch bucket from the saddle horn, and divided the remnants of my lunch between the two of us.

"Mrs. Monday, we'll think what to do," I said after persuading her to eat while she sipped the coffee she had poured into her saucer.

"Mrs. Monday, first I have to ask you a question. Now, you know Mr. Albright is dead." At this, she fell back again on the bed, covering her face with a pillow. I said, "Mrs. Monday? Didn't you know Mr. Albright was dead?"

She lay still. Then her left foot moved slightly, gesturing "yes."

I shifted my attention to her foot. "Mrs. Monday, I think he was murdered."

Now the response was emphatic. "Yes, yes, yes!" her foot said, going up and down.

I stopped and took a deep breath. The foot, expectant and alert, waited, poised for the next question.

"Mrs. Monday, do you know who killed him?"

Nothing. Stillness.

Then, "Mrs. Monday, did Berl kill Mr. Albright?"

"No!" she cried, uncovering her face and sitting up all at once. "I killed him!"

Forgetting the china plate in my lap, I stood up, sending it bouncing onto the dirt floor.

"Oh, Mrs. Monday, you didn't!" I gasped. "How? Why? Oh, Mrs. Monday."

"I'm *rilly* sorry," she said sadly. "I'm *rilly* sorry."

"You tied him up? Put him on the railroad tracks?"

"No!" she said, as astonished as I had been a minute before, "I put a spell on him. Berl didn't want him around no more. He wouldn't stay away and sometimes . . . well, sometimes I wanted him here. So I killed him, I guess." Her expression was a mixture of pride and doleful sorrow.

"How . . . did you do it?" I asked.

"I burned his hat and buried the ashes. I wasn't sure,

though, the spell would take, since he never wore the hat."

Although I felt very tired by then, I told her I would come to see her again before I left White Star to go home for the summer.

So the question remains: Who killed Mr. Albright? Berl? The Constables? Mr. Carrington? I don't know whom to trust.

Lucy

February 15, 1912
At the Constable's

Dear Diary,

Mr. Sully shook his head all the way through our conversation this morning. When I said, "Mr. Sully, Mr. Albright's been murdered," he said, shaking his head, "It doesn't seem likely." Then I said, "Mr. Sully, I have to know if you left a piano under the poplar trees in the school yard just before Christmas." He shook his head firmly and said, "Miss Richards, I never even thought of it."

That leaves the Constables. I'll not mention this to them, but when Mr. Carrington comes this evening with Sheriff Ponder, I'll tell them about the piano. If I had done so sooner, Mr. Albright's life might have been saved.

Right before Mr. Sully left, he said, "I tell you what, Miss Lucy, the day that teacherage is built, I'll be there to help. I'll be right there. You tell Christobel. I'll be at that raising."

When I told Christobel, she turned away so quickly I couldn't see her face. She didn't say a word.

Lucy

February 17, 1912
At the Constable's

Dear Josh,

I had a nightmare last night. I dreamed I was on a train, and I saw a woman's body rolling, rolling slowly, down an incline toward the track. I felt the slight, terrible jar as it passed over the body. Then I knew the woman was me.

I have hardly slept since I found what was left of Mr. Albright that clear, cold day on the way home from school. Then, I tried not to look at his head, but when I close my eyes at night, it is there before me.

Lucy

February 17, 1912
At the Constable's

Dear Diary,

Mr. Carrington and Sheriff Ponder treated my information in the strangest manner. When I told Mr. Carrington a piano had been mysteriously left on the school grounds just before Christmas, he merely raised his eyebrows. I said, "Mr. Carrington, that piano was stolen from the railroad."

He said, "Well, I'll just have to check the bill of lading. We've lost a dining room suite, six chairs, four churns, a boxcar full of hams. But I don't remember a piano. I'll have to look into that." His Adam's apple settled, putting a period to the statement. The two of them turned to walk away. "Sheriff Ponder," I said, "just a minute. Mr. Albright was murdered!"

"Wal now, Miss Lucy. Didn't know you was a detective," he said.

"Sheriff Ponder, his hands had been tied together over his head and untied before I found him. You must have seen the marks," I said firmly.

He turned as if to leave, and then turned back again. He put one hand on each side of the door jam, leaning in a little. "If that's the case, Miss Richards, you'll have to explain how lying there with his arms over his head, it was cut clean off without cuttin' off both arms."

That had not occurred to me. Speechlessly, I watched them leave. But just now I held my wrists as if they were tied together at waist level and found it was quite easy to raise my hands above my head and lower them again to my waist. When Jim Ponder returns, I'll show him this can be done.

I am relieved he knows about the piano. I don't want a stolen one. But, oh, how the children love their music lessons!

Lucy

February 18, 1912
At the Constable's

Dearest Sweetheart,

You must know by now that a week ago I found Olin Albright dead, his body face-up (except there was no face) just outside the railroad tracks; his severed head, a bloody, garbled thing, between the rails. The sheriff has ruled it an accidental death, but I do not believe it. Were his hands, unmistakably evidencing deep rope marks, accidentally bound, too?

Bob, there are things that go on here that I must tell you about. I had planned to write, but your letter came today, saying your Pa had ordered you home to help with the building of my little house. I will tell you everything when I see you.

Despite the murder (it can only be that), I am happy when I think you will soon be home. And Bob, I think your father likes me. When he looks out over his land or at a saddle or at the poplar trees in the schoolyard, his face is solemn, but when he looks at me, he smiles and his eyes dance.

Although it is three long months until school is out, my class, already quite small, is shrinking. The older students, except for Squint, are absent as often as not, working from sunup to sundown to get more land ready for plowing. The twins, poor babies, are sick again. (Jinks Mayfield says that this time it's worms.) But nothing keeps Loretta Abernathy, my newest student, from school. She comes early and stays late. She wants to learn to read and write and cipher—all at once. I wish you could see her, Bob, as I do. She is in bloom.

Your adoring,
Lucy

February 19, 1912
At the Constable's

Dearest Maggie,

Have you changed? I have. In little ways.

A month ago I stopped wearing my bonnet, and now I am as brown as Loretta Abernathy. While her cheeks look slightly sunburned, mine are freckled.

I am still in love with Bob. I found a dead man on the railroad tracks. I think I may have had his murderer in my classroom. I know a desperate woman who lives by desperate means.

But through all this, I expect you, somehow, to stay the same, to be the Maggie who has always loved my brother. And me.

Your best chum,
Lucy

February 20, 1912
At the Constable's

Dear Josh,

Drawn by some notion of need, dread maybe, I went again to Mrs. Monday's after school today. There was no answer to my knock, but when I pushed the door open, I heard her voice, plaintive and fine, thin as a thread, calling to me to come in. She was in bed, huddled under heavy quilts and a magpie assortment of old clothes. Without a fire the dugout was as damp as the bottom of a well.

"Mrs. Monday, it's cold in here. Let me make a fire," I said.

"That would be real nice," she said faintly, "but I've used up all the wood."

"I'll find something," I said. Outside, I went all the way around the house. There was not a stick of wood. Nor even any small chunks of coal. I broke off a branch of mesquite but, in spite of my care, its long sharp thorns tore at my hands. I walked out back, and in the place where Mr. Sams', cow had been tethered, I gathered some of the dried cowpads that lay about. Inside again, I put the fuel in the stove and lit the fire, and as the darkness was closing in, I lit the oil lamp too. Although there was no corn coffee, I found a little tea and put the kettle on the stove, for comfort. Then I drew my chair close to the bed.

"Miss Richards, without Berl," she paused and sighed a long, shuddering sigh, "I jist don't think I can make it. There's so much I wanted to do for him. And couldn't." The yearning in her voice caught at my heart. The words went on, slow and dreamy, like reeds in the bottom of a creek bed. "He's a good boy, Berl is, only with a terrible temper, like his father's." She raised herself up on her elbow, and her eyes, coming into the small pool of light from the lamp, shone from the dark shadows encircling them. "I had to leave his daddy. He was a rough man, everything about him—his hands, his voice. Why, he walked on the ground itself like he was mad at it." Now her words, desperate to be told, tumbled over one another. "But it were Berl I left him for. One afternoon, I took the money from the sugar bowl in the kitchen of the boarding house where I worked, and we got on a train and rode as far as that money would take us, all the way out here. To White Star."

I added sugar to the tea and handed Mrs. Monday a cup. The dug-out was a little warmer, and she threw off some of her cover.

"Miss Richards, you got to understand that Berl's daddy was a toper. And when he got to drinking, he was downright mean, though he didn't think it. I worked most ever' night, and he'd take Berl to the saloon right across from the stockyards. Berl, pore little fellow, would go to sleep jist about anywhere, his head on a table or curled up on the floor in a corner. Most of the time, Sam would let him be. But if another man come in with his boy, Sam would poke Berl awake with the toe of his boot. 'All right, boy, wake up! Now fight! Atta boy. Fight!' The men would sic the boys on each other like two little cur dogs. Oh, they thought it was great sport, them drunken men, and, most of the time, no harm done. Nothin' more'n a bloody nose or a darkened eye."

Now Mrs. Monday sat up and looked out into the darkness across the room. "But one night, that last night," she said, her words clotted and heavy, as if erupting from an old wound, "that last night, Sam come home with Berl, come with his own little boy slung over his shoulder like a sack of meal, and leaving a trail of blood behind. I was waitin'. He come close, and I smelled the liquor and the sweat and the *rottenness* of him. He was grinning, his lips flattened wide across his teeth. 'Old woman,' he said, 'Berl fit a dawg tonight, and he lost. Yore boy lost.' And he dumped Berl onto the bed and went on back to the saloon. That's how Berl lost his ear lobe. His daddy made him fight a dog!"

At that minute, I wanted to kill his father. Then I knew Berl was capable of murder. Anybody is.

It does seem likely that Berl killed Mr. Albright, but, Josh, was there ever a more cruel story? A more misused little boy? A sadder mother?

Your friend,
Lucy

P.S. The very next day Christobel sent Mrs. Monday some food and a supply of wood.

February 21, 1912
At the Constable's

Dear Katie,

The happiest news! Beginning the middle of March, you have a job in Josh's school for the rest of the year. He drove over yesterday and asked if I thought you would finish out the year for Jewel Kennon, a first grade teacher in Estelline who is expecting. (She had not even told Josh she was married, because married ladies cannot teach out here, or anywhere, I suppose.) I went right ahead and accepted for you! I told Josh you would be thrilled. Your salary will be forty-four dollars a month, two dollars more than mine.

Josh thought you would live in Estelline since it is eleven and a half miles from White Star, but I told him that I would find a way for us to live together in our own little house. And I will. I have a plan.

Aren't we the luckiest girls in the world? It's as if we hold out our hands, and good fortune falls into them like ripe, purple plums from a tree.

Be on the train March 5th. That's a Tuesday. Bob and I will meet you in Estelline.

Love,
Lucy

February 22, 1912
At the Constable's
Dear Mr. Sully,

It's a comfort to know that if the piano proves to be stolen goods and is reclaimed by the railroad, you will donate another piano to the school. Here music is not a luxury; it is a necessary beauty, a constant source of pleasure.

Thank you again, Mr. Sully. What a blessing you are.

Affectionately,
Lucy

THE TRAIN TO ESTELLINE

Dear Katie,

I believe that my plan is going to work out. I found a perfect motorcar for you and me. And, I hope, a way to buy it as well. It's a Brush Runabout, a spiffy little car with shock absorbers, a top, a storm front, gas lights, a generator, and a box of tools. Ruby Mills' father is selling it because his wife opposes a car. (Christobel says Mrs. Mills has not slept in her husband's bed since he bought it.) Mr. Mills has kept it in his barn most of the time (slept there too I suppose), and it looks brand new. It has a single cylinder engine, and it can travel forty-eight miles on one gallon of gasoline.

I made an appointment with Mr. White, the president of the Estelline bank, this afternoon. He sat behind his big desk and smiled and smiled at me. I told him I wanted to borrow two hundred and sixty-five dollars. Then his smile vanished and he sat up straight in his chair.

"That's a good amount of money for a young lady to need," he said.

"My sister Katie is going to be teaching in Mr. Arnold's school this spring, and we have to have a motorcar so she can drive back and forth from White Star everyday to teach."

Mr. White chuckled. Then he laughed. Then he held his hand over his side and laughed louder. People in the bank looked at him. And me. I did not know why he was laughing. I waited until he had stopped. "I've prepared a statement explaining how I plan to repay the bank," I said, glad I had worn my blue skirt and my sailor blouse, feeling businesslike as I handed him the sheet of paper over which I had labored so long. Mr. White did not look at the paper.

"Miss Richards, can you drive?" he asked.

I shook my head. "No," I said.

At that he began to laugh again. "You want to buy a car and can't . . . ," he laughed, interrupting himself, "can't . . . , ha ha, can't even, ha, drive it!" But then as suddenly as he had begun to laugh, he stopped. "Your daddy will have to go on the note," he said, his mouth again in a line as straight as a ruler.

"My father is dead," I told him, feeling always when I say the words as if Papa had committed some slightly impolite act by dying.

Then Mr. White said, "I understand you been stepping out with the Sully boy." The calculating way it was said made me know it was a business comment rather than a friendly one.

Looking across the desk at him, I thought about what he had just said. When he was not laughing, he looked *orderly*. His hands carefully rested on his wide oak desk, his jewel links shining on cuffs protruding just beyond his coat sleeves. His hair, neatly combed to the front, failed to hide his neatly receding hairline. Only the two black moles on the right side of his nose looked casual, as if carelessly thrown there. He began to leaf through the papers that had been lying under his hands. His neck and his face flushed red, and I realized I had been staring.

Abruptly, he jumped to a banker's question. "Miss Richards, you got a brother who would go on the note?"

"Yes," I said, "I have. You just send the papers up to Oklahoma today." I scribbled George's address on a sheet of paper and stood up. "My brother will be glad to go on

my note!" I said, flinging the words over my shoulder as I
left.

Mr. White is not a fair man. I do not relish the thought
of doing business with him. But I think we will soon
have a car.

Lucy

February 24, 1912
At the Constable's

Dear George,

I'm sure Mama has written you that Katie is practically on her way out here right now. But you may not
know she will be teaching in Josh Arnold's school for the
rest of the year. It is for this reason that we need an automobile. Then we can live together in the splendid new
teacherage the White Star community is going to build
for us March 1st, and Katie can drive in to school every
day.

The bank in Estelline will loan us the money for the
car provided you will sign the note. Here is the way I pro-
pose to repay the bank:

Total cost of Brush Runabout_____$350.00
Down payment from my savings_____$ 85.00
Remainder owed Estelline bank_____$265.00
Payments in April and May (total amount)_$ 60.00
Amounts paid in June, July and August____$ 0.00
Amount of payment beginning in September and
    each month thereafter_____$ 30.00
Final payment in July of 1913_____$ 3.90
Total amount of interest, at 20%, paid bank
_____$ 38.90

If either or both of us should marry before May, we would sell the automobile and, after paying off the remainder of the note, divide any profit between us. Isn't this a sound plan? If you agree, sign the note and send it right back. We need the car immediately.

George, do things go well with you? And with Inez? I am glad you stopped by Bonham on your way to New Orleans. Mama said Inez is dark and beautiful.

Love,
Lucy

February 25, 1912
At the Constable's

The Trustees of the White Star School
White Star, Texas
@ The White Star Feed and Seed Store
Dear Sirs:

I am disappointed that you did not approve the plans I drew up for the teacherage, but I understand your reason. You are quite right to assume the school will grow and to plan for that accordingly.

As I understand it, you will simply build another classroom on the present one and allow my sister and me to live in it until it is needed. Certainly, I could prepare my meals on the heating stove, and it is true that both the well and the privy are already in place.

But I had hoped that the building might be more of a home than a future classroom. Would you consider, perhaps, some kind of temporary inside walls so that the rooms, at least the bedroom and the kitchen, might be separate. And I would like a closet in the bedroom.

Sincerely,
Lucinda Eliza Richards

THE TRAIN TO ESTELLINE

February 25, 1912
At the Constable's

Dear Diary,

The White Star board of trustees needs a woman on it. If those men were building a barn, they'd not skimp on a thing. I wish I could talk it over with Christobel, but she is off the other side of Estelline, nursing a little boy with measles *and* chicken pox.

But it doesn't matter what the trustees decide. Bob will soon be here, and my sister Katie, too. I am surprised at the happiness I feel when I think about Katie. Here, her reputation will not matter, and the two of us, living together, will not just be sisters, but dear, dear friends.

Whatever the trustees decide about the house, I never once thought I would one day have so much, be so happy!

Lucy

February 26, 1912
At the Constable's

Dear Josh,

A chapter is over and done with. Since you were a part of it from the beginning, I know you will be as saddened as I by the news I heard this morning.

The Samses came late to school. Standing just inside the door, waiting until we had finished the pledge and had sung "America, the Beautiful," they looked so solemn, I knew something was wrong. Then Big 'Un (the students persist in calling George by his nickname) said, "Mrs. Monday's dead!"

"Dead!" I said, astonished by the news. After all, I had seen her just last week.

"Pa found her," Little 'Un said. "Dead in bed."

At that, Oda Ray began to rock back and forth in her desk. "Dead in bed. Dead in bed," she chanted, enjoying the rhyme.

"Oda Ray," I said sharply, "dead is . . ." but how to explain the word to a six-year-old. I began again. "Oda Ray, if you're dead, you're . . ." Helplessly, I stopped again. While we pondered the word, a bee buzzed solemnly in through the barely-opened window and, miraculously, out again.

Then Jinks Mayfield stepped in. "Dead is gone," she chirped.

"Gone!" said Ida Fay in disbelief. She began to cry. Oda Ray joined her twin in the crying. "Gone," Jinks Mayfield echoed mournfully, awed by the effects of her pronouncement. Then, she too began to sob.

"Cripes!" Little 'Un said.

"Jesus!" said Big 'Un.

The Samses looked out the window. Tears ran down Loretta Abernathy's cheeks. My eyes began to fill.

I wondered what we mourned. The twins' loss of innocence? Mrs. Monday's death? The Samses' apparent stoicism?

Suddenly, the classroom seemed far too small. "Recess, recess!" I called, startling the students. And myself. Obediently, they filed from the room. "Just a minute, George," I said. "I want to talk to you."

I sat at my desk and folded my hands in the manner of a bank president. George sat at his desk and tried to cross his legs. The desk was too small. He turned sideways and crossed them. Together, we collected ourselves.

"What was the matter with Mrs. Monday?" I asked.

"Pa don' know. Hungry maybe. Sick."

"Brokenhearted," I added. "Surely that!"

"Pa says that Berl 'ull turn mean when he hears it. Meaner'n a snake," George said.

"Maybe he will. Maybe he won't," I said, sounding, even to my own ears, just like the Samses.

"Pa says that when she died she was holding a letter in her hand. Pa said to give the letter to you."

Incredibly, he pulled a crumpled letter from his pocket. Berl had written:

Dear Ma,

In about a month, I can send you sum money. Til then if you need any thing ask Miss Richurds. If enybody has a kind heart she does. I no she will not let you down or me ether.

Your son,
Berl

But I did let her down. I should have gone back the next day. Although I did not know she was sick, I knew she was cold. I think my own happiness caused me to forget about her.

This has put a damper on everything. Somehow, the teacherage and the motorcar, even Katie's arrival, are not so important today.

Your friend,
Lucy

P.S. The Samses made a coffin and buried Mrs. Monday that same day, not too far from her dugout. George said they had to hurry because she had been dead two days, and without a camphor cloth over it, her face had turned black as coal.

February 27, 1912
At the Constable's

Dear George and Inez,

Both your telegram and the draft for three hundred and fifty dollars came today. There was never a more generous brother in the world. Or sister!

When I read the wire, I was sitting on my bed at the Constable's, and I let out a war whoop that could be heard for miles! I danced a victory dance throughout the empty house and then sat down and wrote Mr. White, the president of the bank, saying I had made other arrangements for the financing of the car.

The Constables were all outside; Mr. Constable harrowing a field, Squint stacking and burning brush, Cable and Jonathan cutting and loading up the lumber for my new house. (I hope it wasn't stolen.) They all gathered to hear my news. Even the girls, visiting Susan at the weaning house, heard the commotion and came running.

I read the telegram out loud to them, and when I got to your offer to buy us a Marmon, if we'd have it, instead of the Brush Runabout, they couldn't believe their ears! Neither could I. But we don't need anything as big and grand as a Marmon. The little Brush Runabout suits us and the countryside to a "t." And it's so light that if we should get stuck in the mud, which seems unlikely since it never rains in West Texas, Katie and I could push it out ourselves.

When Cable goes to see Ruby tonight, he will take the draft over to her father, and when Bob gets home, he will drive the car out to us.

Again, dear George and Inez, thank you for your loving generosity.

Always,
Lucy

February 28, 1912
At the Constable's

Diary,

A flurry of noise in the hall, my door flung open, and Katie standing there, smiling and calm.

"Oh, Katie," I cried. "How did you get here?"

She looked over her shoulder at Josh standing just behind her. I hugged her. She smelled like honeysuckle and pine and roses. "Katie, you've come early! I'm glad you've come. I can't believe it!" I turned to Josh. "How did you find her?" I asked.

"I saw her stepping off the train," Josh said. "And I knew she was your sister. Jim Ponder was with me, and he thought it was you. 'What's Miss Richards doing, getting off the Wichita Falls train?' he asked."

Then Cable and Jonathan came in, bringing her trunk. They put it on the floor next to mine. "That one has all my clothes," Katie said, "and some linens. There's another one," she said, smiling at the Constables. Putting their hats back on their heads, they went out to get the second one. "Wait until you see what Mama sent out here for our house, Lucy. Quilts and a pressing iron and dishes. The prettiest dishes you ever saw."

I hugged her again. "Katie, aren't you tired? You don't look a bit tired," I said. And standing there in a dove gray dress, trimmed in black braid, holding an umbrella to match, she looked clean and shiny, as if she had just stepped from her bedroom. Only her hair, slightly ruffled, a tendril fallen forward over her shoulder, showed the effects of her long journey.

"I was in the new electric lighted sleeper," Katie said. "I slept all night."

The Constables brought in the second trunk. They took off their hats again. Jonathan looked at the toe of his boot. Cable looked at Katie. Amy and Amanda stood in the doorway, looking at my sister.

"If you don't mind my saying so, you've got the prettiest hair I ever saw," Amy said.

Katie stood in the sun that came through the windows. The light brought out the gold and copper colors in it. I had never known it was so beautiful.

"I'll help get supper on the table," I said to Amanda and Amy. "Katie, you rest a while."

"No," Cable said. "You visit with your sister. Me and Jonathan will help." As they went down the hall, I heard Cable's voice again. "Professor, you're staying for supper. Now we won't take 'no' for an answer."

"Sit here, Katie," I said, turning down the bedspread and plumping up the pillows. "Lean back. In this house, we sit on the beds in the daytime. Everybody does."

Katie arched her eyebrows, but she sat down and leaned back. "Oh, Lucy, I am glad to be out here. Mama is such a fussbudget. Worry, worry, worry. That's all she ever does."

"Well, she can't fuss over you way out here. We're going to have a wonderful time," I promised.

I began to tell her about my students and the teacherage and Bob. About the car. She blinked once or twice and then, as if surprised, she opened her eyes wide, closed them, and was asleep.

At the supper table that night, Cable and Lacey outdid each other, telling Katie outlandish stories of tramps and tarantulas and wild horses. Even Mr. Constable, usually silent throughout the meals, entered into the fun.

After supper Josh said, "Walk with me to the car, Lucy."

Snatching up a throw from the horsehair sofa, I wrapped it around my shoulders and walked outside with Josh. Knowing he was as fond of the Constables as I, I asked him if he believed they stole from the railroad. He said there was some talk of it. "Jim Constable's neighbors say he swings a long rope. Some say he will steal a cow, butcher it, and send half of it back the next day," Josh said.

"What about the railroad?" I asked. "Would he steal from the railroad? What about Mr. Albright?"

The slight furrow between Josh's green eyes deepened. "I'd stake my life that not a one of the Constables laid a hand on Albright," he said slowly. "About the railroad, I just don't know. I've never seen any evidence of it."

A light breeze swept between us, soft-lifting the shock of black hair that fell over his forehead. I smiled.

"What is it?" he asked.

"I'd like to read that poem," I said. "By Mr. Keats. The one you said was written for me."

"It goes like this," Josh said, and he began to recite in a slow, teasing voice:

You say you love; but with a voice
  Chaster than a nun's, who singeth

The soft Vespers to herself
  While the chime-bell ringeth-
    O love me truly!

" That's the first of it. You can read the rest for yourself,"
he said, going to the front of his car to crank it. Effortlessly, he wound it up. The motor started.

"Go on," I said, irritated by the lines he had spoken.
"What's the next verse?"

Josh, not bothering to open the door of his car, climbed
over it into the seat. I could not see his eyes, but I could
feel them looking at me. He began the second verse, his
Tennessee accent barely touching the "r's" in some of the
words:

You say you love; but with a smile
  Cold as sunrise in September
As you were Saint Cupid's nun,
  And kept his weeks of Ember.
    O love me truly!

Josh stepped on the gas pedal. "How do you know how
I love?" I called to him as he drove off into the night. And
I'm not so chaste either, Josh Arnold, I said to him silently. Thinking of Bob, a shiver went down my spine. I
stood outside a few minutes, watching the dark clouds
sweep over the moon, before going inside to talk to Katie.

                                                    Lucy

                              March 1, 1912
                              At the Constable's
Dear Mama,
    You must not worry about Katie. She is just fine. This
morning she was a little nauseated, but I remember how

sick the gypsum water made me when I first came out. We are taking good care of her. Christobel made some chamomile tea for her this morning, which she says is the best thing for her until she gets used to the water.

Every one of the Constables has made her feel right at home. When I came from school today, Katie and Cable went riding, Katie sitting Gambol as if she were born in the saddle. Cable has not taken his eyes off her since her arrival. Mama, I just know that all her troubles are over now.

Tomorrow is Saturday, and we're having the raising for the teacherage. The lumber is already on the ground. The men will work on the building all day, and tomorrow evening the women will come with all the food in the world. And Mr. Abernathy and his brothers, who are quite musical, are going to play for the dance that follows.

And, best of all, Bob will be home.

Love,
Lucy

March 2, 1912
At the Constable's

Dear Diary,

My true love came home today. I heard his car and was out the door and in his arms before he had time to knock. He grinned and his blue eyes danced. "You missed me!" he said. "Come on. Admit it! You missed me!" He picked me up and whirled me around. I put my arms around him and kissed him. Hard. There, Josh Arnold! I thought. See how I love!

"Hello," said Katie softly.

Startled, I stepped back, away from Bob.

"This is my sister," I said. "Katie, you can guess who this is."

"It's Bob," she said solemnly, holding out her hand.

"I didn't know you were here," Bob said. "Lucy's been tickled to death that you were coming. And just in time for the teacherage raising!" He looked back over his shoulder toward his car. "I'm on my way out there right now. Pa said they staked it and laid the foundation yesterday. Jimmy brought out the shakes for the roof last night, and this morning he's gone to White Star to pick up the stove." Bob stood for a minute looking at Katie and at me. "You don't look a thing alike," he said. Then "Well, I better be gettin' on. There's lots to do." Suddenly, he seemed uncomfortable. A little shy, I decided, around Katie.

After Bob left, Katie showed me the treasures she had brought—the sheets, a linen tablecloth, silver candlesticks, a Dutch oven, a coffee pot, blue and white enamelware and the prettiest wash basin and pitcher, handpainted with violets. And the quilts! A Wedding Ring, a Texas Star, a Dresden Plate, and a woolen Nine Patch. Clearly, Mama wanted us to be warm.

Aunt Catherine had made rag rugs in softly faded colors, mostly blue. The Sullys had sent over a bed, and Jonathan had made a table. We had no chairs, but we could use the desks from the school. I looked at all the things spread around the room. So much at once. A bounty of things!

While Squint and Cable showed Katie about the farm, I packed. And by early afternoon, I was ready to move.

I walked through the house once more, feeling again the affection I had known there. I saw the place where

Christobel had stood in Mr. Sully's arms. And the room where Petey and I had talked the day Josh brought him home. I will miss them, but I am ready to leave.

Lucy

March 3, 1912
The Teacherage

Dearest Maggie,

I write this letter from my own little house! Can you believe it? I can't. Remember the houses we used to make on the vacant lot next to ours when we were little girls? We'd bend the tall grass over, making arched ceilings for each room, and, for flowers, we would pick the cotton blossoms in the Smiths' field. When they were slowly turning pink, I thought they were the prettiest flowers in the world.

Bob came by to take me to church today, and I insisted that Katie come too. She has not felt well, and I knew the fresh air would be good for her. But, most of all, I wanted the community to meet her. And she charmed them all, even Bob's mother, with her sweet smile and shy manner.

Yesterday was a marvelous day; clear and cold and inviting everybody to step out in it, the kind of day that makes you know spring is on its way. About an hour before sunset, we drove over here with Christobel and the Constable girls. By then the outside walls were up, and the rafters all in place, as well as the lathe that topped them. Mr. Sully, Bob, Jimmy Green, and two of the hands were putting shakes on the roof. Mr. Baldridge, Mr. Sams, and Mr. Abernathy were stuccoing the outside walls. The Constables and Mr. Mayfield, under the direction of the women, were finishing up the interior.

I heard Christobel saying, "Certainly, those girls need a closet in the bedroom. When we need it for a classroom, the kids can hang their coats in there." And Mrs. Sams, who looks like her husband, but with longer hair, said, "There's not a reason in the world why we can't have as good a teacherage as Estelline's. That right, Mr. Arnold?"

"No reason for it not to be better!" Josh said. By sunset it was all finished, all but the whitewashing. And Mr. Sully said he would have that done tomorrow.

While the men finished the teacherage, the women worked in the classroom, getting ready for the hoedown. They put out the baked hams and fried chicken and smoked beef on my desk, and on a sawhorse table they put the angel food and fudge chocolate and pound cakes and the pumpkin, coconut, and Jefferson Davis pies. Mrs. Baldridge, who had said she'd bring the beans, surprised us all by taking two cans of White Swan pork'n beans out of a string bag for her offering. But when we realized Mrs. Mayfield had come empty-handed, hadn't brought a thing, we appreciated the store-bought beans.

The men ate first, and Katie sat right down with them, never realizing most of the women were up, serving. To keep her company, I sat down too and heard Amy Constable whisper to Mrs. Abernathy, "They're from the East," in explanation.

I sat by Bob, and we held hands under the table. Josh argued with Mr. Sully about who should be the next president. Josh wants Mr. Wilson, but Mr. Sully said Mr. Taft would be better for the country. But they agreed with each other about prohibition and argued against Mr. Baldridge on this. Mr. Baldridge got so mad he had to go outside to cool off.

Before everybody had finished, the Abernathy's tuned up with a new song called "The Brown Girl," and pretty soon all the desks were outside on the ground, and everybody was dancing. Most of the time I danced with Bob, but I danced with others too. When they played "Anna Laurie," Mr. Sully asked me to dance. Oh, Maggie, the way that man watches Christobel Constable! It's plain as day he loves her. Lacey Constable, who has the kindest heart, asked Mrs. Sully to dance, but she said she was still in mourning and wouldn't.

Hall County is dry, but at a hoedown you'd never know it. The men were all drinking. And some of the women!

Josh Arnold missed only one dance. That was when he and Cable Constable got into a fight over whether or not a black man has a soul. Josh said only a stupid man would think a black man didn't have one. Cable had to call him on that so they went outside to fight. But pretty soon they were back inside, Cable declaring the professor was right, since he was right about most things. Josh can get most people over to his way of thinking.

My house looks beautiful right now. The Texas Star quilt is on the bed, the rag rugs are down, and the pitcher with violets is filled with purple juniper berries. The room is still a little empty, but so spacious. We will add to it, but only with things which are truly beautiful.

Maggie, do not let your life slip through your fingers. By that I mean, don't pine always for George. Out here, there are fine men who would appreciate and love you. And there are so many more of them than women.

Now that I have my own house, think about coming out here for a visit. Write me that you'll come before summer.

Your best chum,
Lucy

March 5, 1912
The Teacherage
White Star

Dearest Aunt Catherine,

Yesterday Carlos' family came for him!

I had gone to the well to draw water when I glanced out into the gathering darkness and saw . . . something. I did not know what it was, but it seemed as if the landscape had been intruded upon by a cluster of forms, somewhat like rocks, of various heights and taller than they were wide. So motionless were they that they seemed to be a part of the land, as if they had somehow been washed out of it. Silently questioning the darkness, I walked out toward them, and still they did not move. Then, "*Carlos? Donde esta Carlos?*" a man's voice, at once gentle and compelling, came from the darkness, making me know it was Carlos' family and that they had come for him.

I ran to the schoolhouse and told Carlos. He dropped the book he was reading and bounded, like a gazelle, out of the classroom and down the steps.

In a little while, he reappeared. "Senorita, I go with my family," he said.

"But Carlos, what about school? What about your education?"

"I must go tomorrow," he said. "It is necessary. You know I must go."

Then who would clean the schoolhouse, I wondered. Chop the wood? Selfish questions, I told myself. "Of course you must go with your family," I said. "We'll miss you, but of course you must go." Parroting a phrase Carlos often used whenever I left, *"Vaya con Dios,"* I told him.

At dawn the next morning I looked out my window to see Carlos and his family just beginning their long trek. His father carried a huge bundle on his back and his mother a smaller one. Carlos leaned over and swung a small child across his shoulders, straightening slowly under his burden. Then the little family turned their backs on the schoolhouse and began their long walk toward the North, looking for work.

The wind rose and the sand began to blow. I stood watching them, knowing that in just a few minutes Carlos would be gone forever. Impulsively, I ran next door and into the schoolroom. Grabbing up the book he had just put down, I ran after him calling, "Carlos! Carlos!"

Finally, he heard me, for he stopped, turned around, and began to walk in my direction.

"I want you to have this," I said, handing him *Moby Dick.* "You can read it again and again. Carlos, whatever happens, you musn't forget how to read."

"Always, I will read. The book is a present more wonderful than any I have had," he said earnestly. "I will read others. I will read many of them."

"Carlos!" His father's voice was demanding. *"Vamos!"*

I watched Carlos ease his little sister across his back again and gradually disappear with his family into the swirling sand.

So Carlos has become a wanderer again. Did he always know that this was his destiny? Is that why he loved this book so much? Aunt Catherine, I am glad he has it, gladder still that he can read it.

Katie sends her love and says she will write when she has a little time.

Love,
Lucy

March 6, 1912
The Teacherage

Dear Christobel,

Katie and I enjoyed the baked ham and lima beans that you sent out by Squint. We have not cooked all week long, thanks to you and the girls.

Our little house is arranged nicely, and already we feel quite at home. Just now everything takes place in the middle of the room close to the stove, but when the weather warms, we'll move the bed under the windows and arrange a small parlor at one end of the room.

Since Carlos has left, I am doubly glad that Katie is here with me. When my pupils all leave, the deserted classroom moans and creaks all night long as if it too misses Carlos.

I am a little concerned about Katie. Could you send another remedy by Squint? She has not yet become accustomed to the water and is sometimes nauseated, even when she drinks chamomile tea. But by the time I'm finished with my teaching each day, she usually feels more like her old self. Then she enjoys riding Gambol, with H.H. following closely at her heels. Already she rides better than I.

Bob and Jimmy Green are bringing the Runabout on Friday, and Bob will teach us to drive on Saturday. Don't be surprised if you hear our car on the canyon bridge. We might drive over for a visit!

Your friend,
Lucy

March 7, 1912
The Teacherage

Dear Josh,

When you brought out all those books for Katie and me, you must have depleted your library. How many do you have? When we learn to drive, could we pay you a visit? I would love to see all your books, in their splendid leather bindings, shining from the dark shelves.

At home we had so few books—the Bible, Shakespeare, *Little Women*. But we had an excellent town library. In their house, the Constables have a patent-medicine almanac, a mail order catalogue and old newspapers, but no books except for the Bible. Not even the Sullys have many. So as far as books go, you seem to be the richest man in Hall County.

We've been making good use of them. We moved our bed close to the stove, and each night after supper we add more wood, and then we sit in bed and read. In spite of the poem you mistakenly chose for me, I have developed a great fondness for John Keats. Katie likes Lord Byron, and sometimes we read *Don Juan* to each other. Wasn't he wicked?

Katie is learning to drive on Saturday so she can be at your school bright and early Monday morning. She appears to be quite calm about this, her very first position, but she is really very excited, too excited to sleep. I often wake in the middle of the night to find her pacing back and forth. Sometimes, she continues this for an hour or more before quietly slipping back into bed.

Sincerely,
Lucy

March 10, 1912
The Teacherage
White Star, Texas

Dear Maggie,

Bob came over about noon today to teach Katie to drive. Wearing his chaps, his broad brimmed hat, and his heavy roping gloves, he looked more as if he were getting ready to break a horse than give a driving lesson. Katie took right to the driving. She watched Bob like a cat, copying his every move.

He cranked the car; the engine started. Then Katie tried it, and the engine turned over just as fast for her. Bob began to explain the mechanics of the car to Katie, but she put her hand on his arm, opened her eyes wide and said, "I want to drive it; I don't want to build it." Bob broke into a loud laugh, and I realized how seldom I ever hear him laugh out loud. But he is almost always smiling.

Katie climbed into the driver's seat and looked at him. "Climb in. Hold on," she said.

Chuckling, Bob climbed in beside her, and she drove in rather jerky circles round and round the school house. After about twenty minutes of circling, she stopped the car. "If there is a road out here, I'd like to practice driving on it," she said to Bob.

When they drove off toward Estelline, Katie was managing to stay in the middle of the road, as far as I could tell. By the time they returned in the late afternoon, they were both convinced Katie would have no trouble driving to Estelline on Monday.

I am not surprised. Katie is so quick and graceful. Any motion comes naturally to her. Sitting, walking, even sleeping, it's as if her body knows only a natural grace. Oh Maggie, you know how clumsy I've always been. Falling, bumping into things, stumbling over my own feet. However, I do believe I can learn to drive. It looks quite simple.

While they were gone, I put the linen tablecloth and candles on the table, and I made a skillet supper of chicken and tomatoes. I asked Bob to stay, and was disappointed when he said his mother was expecting him for supper. I walked with him to his car, enjoying his amusement at Katie's driving. He said a tumbleweed had blown across her path, and she had stopped so suddenly that he was nearly thrown through the storm window. On the other hand, when she had seen a cow in the road, she had stepped on the accelerator and would have run over it had Bob not taken the wheel.

Maggie, they like each other, and I am glad. I was afraid Bob would not approve of Katie, but out here she is a different person.

Love,
Lucy

March 11, 1912
The Teacherage

Dear Diary,

Our beautiful little Brush Runabout—ruined! I wrecked it myself. Even now I can't believe the shining little car is now a misshapen pile of metal that might be past repairing.

But what really worries me is Katie. I feel sick about Katie.

This morning we drove into White Star to attend services there. It was a quiet day and almost warm. Katie had put on my navy skirt and white georgette blouse, the blouse straining against her bosom as she buttoned it. I teased her; "Katie, if you gain another pound, you won't be able to wear my blouse." Katie's expression, as she crossed her arms protectively over her breasts, was desperate. "Katie, I was teasing you. You have a perfect shape. You're not a bit too fat," I said.

But my thoughtless remark silenced both of us until we had driven onto the church grounds. Then she turned to me. "Lucy, there's something I just have . . ." she began, but I did not want to hear what Katie had to say, and the choir had begun its first hymn. "Come on, Katie. We'll be late," I said, and we hurried into the church.

Mrs. Sully beamed at Katie after church, Katie's quiet "Yes ma'ams" and "No ma'ams" clearly music to her ears. Oh, if you only knew Katie, I thought. If you only knew that Katie, more than me, more than anybody, does just what she wants to do, then you'd not be so quick with your smiles.

Mrs. Sully asked us to Sunday dinner, but Katie said she had to prepare her lessons for Monday. Bob walked us to the car but, supposing that Katie had spoken for both of us, he did not urge me to come out to the ranch.

All afternoon Katie was quiet, but more than quiet, *sad*. I thought of how lonely I had been when I had first come out. It's that, I thought. It's no more than that. Katie's homesick.

"Katie, teach me how to drive, and we'll drive over to the Constable's. Cable would dearly love to see you," I said.

She brightened immediately. "Would he, Lucy? Do you think he really would?"

The little car, shining in the sun, looked so pretty when we went outside that I'd have been content just to admire it for awhile, but Katie was in a hurry. "All right, Lucy, crank it up," she said.

I did and, miraculously, it started. We circled the school several times and then, even though the car's pace was not quite smooth, I drove across the pasture and onto the wagon road that led to the Constable's.

"It's easy," I said to Katie. "All you have to know is that one pedal makes it go and the other one makes it stop." I stole a glance toward her. She was smiling, and I was glad I had suggested the visit to the Constable's.

Then I remembered the canyon bridge! "Katie, can you drive across the bridge?" I asked.

"I'm not sure, but . . . here comes another car!" she gasped. And astonishingly, there was another one, about one hundred yards away, headed straight toward us.

For an instant, I started to apply the brake. The car was now about fifty feet away. Josh's car! There was not enough time to stop. I stepped on the accelerator and took to the pasture on my left, away from the canyon bridge coming up on the right, just as Josh swerved off the road. We were again on a collision course. I turned the wheel to the right, and Josh turned his car in the same direction. It was as if the cars had become magnets, unable to escape each other. Just before the crash, I glanced at Katie. Her mouth was open in a soundless expression of surprise. "Hold on!" I cried to her and to myself just before the crash.

Afterwards, I sat stunned, listening to my heart beat in a vast silence, broken only by the sound of the wheel that rolled crazily off across the pasture. "Dadblastit," Josh said, climbing quickly from his car. "Are you all right, Lucy?" he asked, helping me down from the car.

"Katie, oh Katie, look what I've done," I said to my sister.

"Are *you* all right?" Josh asked as he helped Katie, trembling visibly, from the car.

"I think so, but oh, just look at our car!"

We stood, the three of us, and looked at it. The right front wheel was in the pasture, at the moment being nosed by a cow, and the left one was bent under the fender. The motor had been pushed back, and half of it was tilted straight up into the air.

Josh's car was hardly scratched.

"Lucy, it's all right. You couldn't help it. Please don't worry," Katie said softly.

"Josh, why didn't you stay on the road? If you had just stayed on the road, this wouldn't have happened!" I said.

"You've been driving all of about ten minutes, and you're standing in the middle of this pasture telling me how to drive. I can't believe any of this. You chased me all over the dadburned pasture! Why, I couldn't get out of your way. You are supposed to stay to the right of an on-coming car!"

"You should have told me that," I said. "Nobody mentioned that."

"If anybody had told me a car would run into me in

the middle of a pasture, I'd have said they were crazy," Josh said, gathering up the tools that were scattered about. He walked around the car, looking at it from every angle. "I think it can be fixed. We'll get the wheels back on and pull it into Estelline. Or, we might put it on a wagon and haul it in. Anyway, I'll ask Otis Lumpkin to look at it and see if he can repair it."

"What will I do about school tomorrow?" Katie asked.

"Oh, I can circle by and pick you up for a few days, until your car's fixed," Josh said. "And I expect Bob Sully would bring you home. Or Cable. Cable bought a Hupmobile this week. I imagine Cable would bring you home."

Cheered somewhat by Josh's estimate of the situation, we got into his car and drove across the bridge and on to the Constable's. When we arrived, the news of our wreck was overshadowed by the Constable's news. Cable had bought Mr. Sully's Hupmobile. Then he had eloped in it, had driven up to Oklahoma to marry Ruby Mills.

What surprised me more than the news of Cable's marriage was Katie's reaction to it. On the way home she said sadly, "Lucy, I was counting on him. I was counting on Cable."

I did not ask her what she meant by that. When I think about what she meant, my throat gets so tight I cannot swallow.

Lucy

March 15, 1912
The Teacherage

Dear Diary,

I've been terrified (now I can bear to write the words!) that Katie was going to have a baby. And with reason!

Her nausea. Her moods. I was so sure of it I even imagined a fuller figure!

But no more. Whatever was troubling her has vanished along with her moodiness and nausea. Now she gets up early and prepares both our breakfasts, humming a little tune deep in her throat and now and then singing out the words. After breakfast she carefully dresses, sometimes trying on two or three garments before finally settling on one, and each morning when she leaves, she looks more beautiful than the morning before.

She, this new Katie, has thrown herself into teaching, and she works quite late. Last night it was almost seven when she came home. I flew out to Bob's car, insisting he join us for supper. Then he seemed so tired throughout the meal that I took pity on him and sent him home early. Just before he left I thanked him. "You've been so patient," I said, "with Katie's schedule. But she shouldn't keep you waiting every day. I'll talk to her."

"Wait, Lucy! Don't do that. The car will be ready soon. I don't mind waiting for her. I'm glad to do it." He was so insistent that I promised to say nothing to Katie.

I was disappointed when he kissed me once and left, but nothing can dampen the euphoria I feel knowing that Katie is not a fallen woman and will not be an outcast. And our family will not be disgraced.

Thankfully,
Lucy

March 16, 1912
The Teacherage

Dear Aunt Catherine,

H.H. had been gone all day when a strong smell floated through the window. Just when I realized the smell was that of a skunk, I heard the whimpering sounds a dog makes when it is in trouble. That could not possibly be H.H., I thought. He never cries. But it was!

I looked outside and saw the most pitiful dog, shivering, his tail between his legs, his ear torn and bleeding. When he saw me, he crawled, still whimpering, a few feet toward me, but he seemed to know he was not fit company and stopped. He lay there, whining.

When Bob and Katie came, Bob said, "You'll just have to leave him alone until it wears off."

"Oh, but just look at him. Look at his ear!" Katie said. "We've got to help him"

"Bob, can't we do something for him. He's so pitiful," I said, adding my pleas to Katie's.

"The only thing I know will deodorize a skunk is tomatoes. Ma's got plenty, and I guess I could go home and get some."

I hugged his neck. "Oh, Bob thank you!" I said.

Bob went to get a half a dozen cans of tomatoes while Katie and I drew enough water for several baths. It took the three of us an hour or more, but by bedtime H.H. was in his accustomed place on the floor by my bed, happily dozing away, and now and then opening his eyes to look up at me with an expression of gratitude and affection.

The next morning when Josh came for Katie, he lost his temper when we told him about H.H. "Well, you're going to have to watch him. You can't take this lightly," he said sternly. "In Tennessee, people have more sense than to fool around with a dog that's been bitten by a skunk. Why I'd rather climb a thorn tree than fool with anything that might be rabid. You just watch and see he doesn't get sick." After he had assured himself that the wound had been carefully cleaned, he calmed down. "Well, old fellow, I think you're going to be all right," he said, patting H.H. on his aristocratic head.

Josh is one of H.H.'s most ardent admirers. You would love him too. He is both gentle and intelligent—a steadfast companion.

Love,
Lucy

P.S. You might wonder why Katie is being driven back and forth to school. We had a small mishap in the Runabout, but it is now being repaired and in a week or so will be as good as new.

March 17, 1912
The White Star Teacherage
To: The Trustees of the White Star School Community
    @ The White Star Feed and Seed Store
Dear Sirs:

Our most urgent need at the present time is a school library. Not even Estelline has a library. Therefore, in this important area of education, White Star could take the lead. This would not only enrich the lives of our students, but the lives of all those who live here.

Although a substantial collection takes years to acquire, we can begin one now. Accordingly, I am requesting your permission to have a supper at the school in order to raise money with which to begin a school library.

I believe that with the proceeds from such an event, we could purchase twenty-five or thirty books.

Sincerely,
Lucinda Eliza Richards

March 20, 1912
The White Star Teacherage

Dear Parents:

You are invited to a program at the school on April the third at six o'clock in the evening. The purpose of the program will be:

A. To entertain the parents with songs and dances the students have learned throughout the year.

B. To raise money for a school library with a supper immediately following the program (25 cents for adults and 15 cents for children).

I know that you will take pride in the knowledge that this occasion will mark the beginning of an excellent library for both the students and the community.

Sincerely,
Lucinda Eliza Richards

March 23, 1912
The White Star Teacherage

Dear Mr. and Mrs. Abernathy,

I shall certainly respect your wishes that Loretta and Bucy not be asked to dance on the program Saturday night. However, in folk dancing only the hands of the partners touch, and, therefore, I do not see how this could possibly lead to adultery. With this in mind, I hope you will reconsider your decision.

Sincerely,
Lucinda Eliza Richards

March 25, 1912
The White Star Teacherage

Dear Mrs. Baldridge,

Although I am sorry that you do not have the time to make the twins' costumes, I understand that you have other duties that demand your time and energy. If you will furnish the yellow and brown broadcloth for their sunflower dresses, I will make them myself.

Sincerely,
Lucinda Eliza Richards

March 27, 1912
The White Star Teacherage

Dear Mrs. Sams,

I agree that when one has seven children (and four of these over eighteen), 25 cents per person is too expensive. Therefore, a fee of only 15 cents per person will be charged to those with three or more children over eighteen.

Sincerely,
Lucinda Eliza Richards

March 28, 1912
The Teacherage

Dear Josh,

Katie and I appreciate your invitation to come for supper, but this is not possible until after the library program is over. I am doing a million things for it.

Would you please make a list of about twenty-five or thirty books which you would choose for the nucleus of a library? The school already has a copy of *David Copperfield*. (I gave the copy of *Moby Dick* to Carlos when he left.) Josh, I would appreciate this more than I can say. I am glad you are coming to the program. Katie and I are looking forward to seeing you.

Lucy

March 31, 1912
The Teacherage

Dear Diary,

I had heard "Have You Ever Been to Texas in the Spring" and "Wild Prairie Flowers, We" a thousand times, but when we had our costume rehearsal, the songs sounded as fresh as when I first heard them.

I had to sew the twins into their costumes because I had not quite finished them. Their petals looked a little wilted, but with all the other costumes, theirs were surprisingly effective.

Bob's visit on Wednesday was the reason I did not finish the twins' costumes. When he brought Katie home, he said, "Lucy, could we talk?"

I said, "Of course. Sit here, and we'll talk while I baste on the petals." After the basting was finished, I tried a sunflower face on Katie, and even with my amateur sewing, she looked just beautiful. Bob sat quietly, looking at her. I could tell he thought she was pretty too. Then he stood up abruptly, or so it seemed to me, and I put down my sewing.

"What did you want to talk about?" I said. "We can talk now."

"Not now," he said, gesturing toward the sewing, the jars of food for the supper already brought in, the costumes stacked in a corner. "Not in the middle of all this."

After he left, I was sorry I had not stopped to listen. He had looked so worried.

"I wonder what Bob wanted to talk to me about," I said to Katie when I got into bed later that night. But Katie, by then, was already asleep.

Lucy

April 2, 1912
The Teacherage

Dear Aunt Catherine,

Our program, for which I wrote the script and arranged the dances myself, is tomorrow. We just had our last rehearsal, and it was perfect.

Each girl was dressed as a wildflower—the twins are sunflowers, Loretta Abernathy is a flutter-mill, Jinks Mayfield is a buttercup, Mary Jane Wilkins a primrose, and Jessie Sams is a lazy daisy, an appropriate choice for her.

The boys refused to be flowers, choosing to be cowboys instead. (I had to rewrite the script completely for this change.) Squint is a lonesome cowboy, George a dying cowboy, Bucy a singing cowboy (Bucy has an exceptionally nice voice), Peep Wilkins a roping cowboy, and on and on. Each had managed to beg or borrow a horse to ride in the program.

As their part begins, each one rides in on his horse and becomes a monument while the rest of us sing "Home on the Range." All of them were recognizable except for the lonesome cowboy and the dying one. It was so hard to tell these two apart that I had Loretta Abernathy introduce Squint and George.

When we added the horses, we had to move the program *and* the piano outside. But this just added to it. The students' voices sound quite beautiful in the clear air and, at the end, when the cowboys all dismount and stand behind the "flowers" to sing "Texas, Our Texas," the scene takes my breath away. It is truly lovely. I wish you could be here tomorrow to see it.

Next week, I'll have all the time in the world, and I plan to spend most of it in Bob's company.

I do love him so!

> Your loving niece,
> Lucy

P. S. Katie said to tell you she is fine. She is so busy with her teaching she has not had time to write.

April 4, 1912

Diary—

I played the piano. When we sang "Texas, Our Texas," I knew they had missed the entire program.

Careless, I thought. Just like Katie. Just like her to be so careless. Then, later, a thousand things went through my mind. The car turning over. Going off into the canyon. Bob and Katie hurt and bleeding, and Bob crawling for help.

"Bad news travels fast," Josh said. "Try not to worry."

We waited for news. All night. All through the night, we waited. Never suspecting. Josh walked up and down. I lay on the bed and waited.

At five, just before dawn's first light, Mr. Sully came with a telegram:

Dear Pa,

Katie Richards and I were married in Tulsa. On our way to a honeymoon in New York. Katie says give Lucy her love.

Bob

Married. The word is weighted and heavy. A stone boiling its way to the heart.

April 1912

Diary,

Up is down and day is night and North is South and love is hate and I don't even know what day it is.

Lucy

April 9, 1912

Dear Diary,

After Papa died, Mama used to say, "Sunday is the lonesomest day. Why is Sunday so lonesome?" Her voice was a keening, like the north wind.

I know what Mama meant. Today is Friday, and I dread the weekend. Most of all, Sunday.

Josh is bringing our car out tonight. *The* car. I won't drive it. Where would I go? A car needs a place, a destination. I do not want to go to the Constable's. Or to Estelline.

I'll ride Gambol tomorrow. H.H. will follow. I know this country. There are no surprises on the prairie.

During recess yesterday, I told Jinks Mayfield I never wanted to hear a Texas song again. She cried.

Mr. Sully rode over on Surprise after school. He was so beautiful.

"Lucy, Miss Richards, I, uh, I always had kinda hoped that you and, uh . . ."

The hurt I felt when I saw Surprise was a hair trigger setting off a rush of anger.

"You were wrong, Mr. Sully."

I hated the sympathy in Mr. Sully's voice and on his face. What good is it?

Lucy

April 10, 1912

Dear Diary,

I rode Gambol out over the prairie. It was still as death. Far off, I saw the Samses in their field. Planting cotton. I turned away to ride along the river. After awhile, H.H. refused to come. He lay down and would not move until we turned back.

I drew some water for a sponge bath. Already, my body has changed, my breasts transformed into something withered and sterile.

I sat on the steps until Josh came. He sat by me. For a long while, he did not say a word. Then, "Lucy, I love you. I always will," he said.

"Always?" I asked, doubting the possibility.

He nodded. A smile played about his lips. He said, "Why Lucy, the first time I saw you, 'I was tangled in thy beauty's web, and snared by the ungloving of thy hand.'"

"Keats," I said.

He nodded. I thought about the other poem. Now I would be "chaster than a nun." I jumped up from the steps. "All right then, marry me, if you love me so much! Marry me!"

I hadn't known the words were there, waiting. I was as startled as Josh. Slowly, he stood up, too. "I'm not going to marry you, not while you're in love with Bob Sully."

"I hate Bob Sully! I hate my sister too. She's going to have a baby! That's why she came out here! That's why Mama wanted her to come. I doubt she even knows whose baby it is. I hate her! I hate them all!"

I was sobbing. I pounded his chest with my fists. "You've got to marry me. You've got to! Oh, please marry me."

Josh shook his head. "No, Lucy. I won't. Not now. It wouldn't be right. For me or for you."

I went in the house and lay down on the bed. After awhile, I heard Josh drive away.

Lucy

April 13, 1912

Diary,

H.H. was under the schoolhouse. He wouldn't come out. The Samses helped me drag him out. His wounds were healed, but something hurt him. He growled at me and refused to eat. He crawled back under the schoolhouse.

Squint Constable said Christobel has gone to Boston to

bring Petey home. I wish she were here, but Squint is
going to ask his father what to do for H.H.

Lucy

April 23, 1912

Diary,

Bob and Katie came today. Bob knocked on my door.
"Lucy, Katie wanted me to bring her home. She wanted
things to be right again. Between the two of you."

"Things will never be right between the two of us."

Katie waited in the car. Bob turned his hat round and
round in his hands. Its brim grew smaller and smaller.
Then the hat was a crumbled, oblong shape.

"We just . . . all of a sudden, we just decided . . ."
Bob began.

I waited. No reparation was possible. I would never be
happy again. Then, "I'm sorry," he said.

Encased in anger as tight as a mummy's wrappings, it
was easy for me not to answer.

Bob stood there, ruining his hat. "Can she come in and
get her things?"

"Certainly." I stood aside, and Bob went to the car and
helped Katie down. Bob stayed at his post by the car.
Katie came up the steps, pausing just inside the door.

"Lucy . . . ," she began.

"Get your things!" I said. Flinching, she covered her
cheek with her hand as if I had struck her there. She
opened her trunk and began to put her clothes inside,
dropping them in, not taking any care, tossing them in.

"You can have the car," she said.

"I don't want it."

She dropped to the side of the bed. Tears ran down her

cheeks. She lifted her skirt and wiped them away with her petticoat, but they kept coming. Slowly, she unbuttoned her skirt and pulled up her blouse. "Lucy, I had to marry. I had to marry somebody. Just look at what's happened to me! Don't you see? I had to marry somebody!"

I looked at her white belly, already slightly swollen. I thought of the streetcar ride, of Katie running off across the pasture. I wondered if the baby belonged to the boy with the red hair.

Sighing, Katie buttoned her blouse and readjusted her skirt.

"Bob doesn't know," she said.

"I'll not tell him," I said disdainfully.

She wiped away the tears again. Bob came in to get her trunk. Following him to the car, she stumbled once and almost fell. Katie, who had always been so graceful, stumbled. Katie's clumsiness shocked me more than her swollen belly.

After they left, I put a hambone and some chicken on a plate. I took it outside and pushed it under the house for H.H. I hoped some of it would be gone by tomorrow.

Lucy

⌾

Josh came. He shot H.H.

⌾

Josh came again this evening. He paced up and down the room. "Why haven't you opened your letters?" he asked, waving them in my face. His voice was harsh. "Lucy, why aren't you eating?" Then, "I had to do it, Lucy." Now his voice was filled with pain; "I'm leaving for Tennessee day after tomorrow. There's some family business to take care of, but a letter from you, just one, and I'd be back in a minute."

Words. Just words. Like a bucket of water on a grass fire. No help at all.

After Josh shot . . . , after he killed H.H., he sat outside my house for three nights. His cigarette glowed red, like a firefly.

April 26, 1912

Diary,

I will write exactly what happened.

Josh got out of the car. I knew why he had come. Poor old H.H. Until now, his tail like a flag, and his feet at the trot stretched up and out, more like an Arabian's than a dog's.

"Josh, listen, he's not mad. He doesn't have rabies. He'll be better tomorrow." Frantically, I whispered the words in Josh's ear.

Josh stooped to look under the schoolhouse. I knelt beside him.

"Come on, H.H. Come on out," I called. We could see his eyes, like two red coals in the dark.

"H.H., come here, boy!" Josh's command was followed by a deep guttural sound from H.H. Not a growl exactly. Then we heard H.H. pick himself up and lunge forward a foot or two, before falling again.

Josh whirled and headed toward his car. I ran to stop him, not looking at the long gun he had taken from the seat. I held on to the arm that carried the gun, but Josh shook me off.

"No, Josh! Josh, please listen!" I shouted, grabbing his arm again.

He took hold of my shoulder with his left hand, shaking me.

"Lucy, I've got to do this!" He spun me off behind him, in the direction of his car, knelt again, and resting his gun on the schoolhouse steps, he fired one shot into the darkness.

"Josh Arnold, I'll never forgive you for this, for what you just did!" I screamed the words at him, "I'll never forgive you!"

Leaving his gun on the steps, he stood up and took both my hands in his.

"Josh, you didn't know what was the matter with him. You could have waited. You didn't know!"

Carefully, he examined my hands, my arms, my face.

"Did he bite you? Break the skin?" he asked.

"You had no right to kill him!" I shouted again. "You had no right!"

Josh said, "I'll bury him. Go on inside."

I stood and watched him pull on a pair of heavy gloves. When he leaned over to drag H.H. out from under the schoolhouse, I went inside and closed the door.

That night, Friday night, I was already in bed, not sleeping but not crying either, when I heard Josh's car. Looking out the window, I saw the dark, uncompromising shape of it, parked in the poplar grove. Just before dawn's first light, I heard the sound of the car's motor as he started it and drove away. He came again on Saturday night. And Sunday. Too restless to sleep, I opened the door and sat on the schoolhouse steps. I could see the tip of his cigarette as he paced up and down beside his car.

He might as well have been a stranger out there, for all I cared.

I did not see Josh again. By now, he's in Tennessee, or well on his way.

Lucy

April 29, 1912

Dear Diary,

At night I sit at my kitchen table. The wind howls through the empty schoolhouse. At times, it sounds like a ship, its mast creaking, its sails straining hopelessly to contain the wind that blows against them. Now a floorboard gives under an unknown weight. A window rattles once, loudly, and is still. The wind assaults the east wall, dies away, and begins a new assault on the west. I have never been so lonely. But, strangely, I do not believe I am alone. Each evening I walk out over the prairie. I look all around, and there is no one there. But someone *was* there. A breath away. A minute ago. *Someone has been there.*

I sit again at the table. Someone is out there now. I feel his eyes on the back of my head. My neck. I turn my head to look, but there is no one there. He has been too fast for me.

In the morning, I open my door. A minute sooner, and I would have seen him. Who is it? Why has he come?

Lucy

⚬

Am I crazy? Is there no one here but me?
Surely, I am crazy. But I am afraid to be crazy.

⚬

May 1, 1912

Diary,

One more week of school. The sun rises. I put on my blue skirt and georgette blouse (Oh, see if it pulls across your breasts), and teach. Two plus four. Columbus discovered. No music. I do not teach music. I have forgotten how.

When the sun goes down, I put on my Mrs. Monday clothes, my roamin' in the gloamin' clothes. I walk across the prairie. "Aunt Catherine, this should never have happened to your sweet Lucy," I cry to the vast blackness of the sky.

May 6, 1912

Diary,

This is the last day of school. Before I say good-bye, I ask the students, "Have any of you seen a stranger around here? Have you seen anyone?" Frowning, they shake their heads. No one answers.

Loretta Abernathy stands up. She slaps her desk with the flat of her hand. "Something's the matter with this school," she says angrily.

"Sit down, Loretta." When she is seated I say to the students, "I have the report cards all ready. When I pass them out, you are free for the summer."

They clap and cheer, but their happiness does not penetrate the wall of glass between them and me. The twins cry when they leave. Jinks Mayfield had wanted a party.

L

Diary,

I am filled with hate, drubbed by it.

I thought there was no room for anything else. I was wrong. There is room for fear. I am afraid. I have never been so afraid.

If I asked Amy Constable to stay with me, she would find out I am crazy. She knows I have been jilted. I do not want her to know I am crazy. I do not want anyone to know.

L

Diary,

I am alone. Except for him. I am beginning to know more. I know when he advances and retreats across the prairie, cleverly appearing and disappearing. Sometimes I almost see a retreating back or a hand holding to my window sill as he scrambles down.

I will go back and forth across the prairie and in and out of my house. Surely, one day I will see him, an instant before he drops down out of sight, a second before he turns away.

If anyone is there.

L

My diary. Writing. I hold on to that.

Diary,

It rained the last week of school. Overnight, the prairie is filled with wide splashes of color—the wildflowers of West Texas. Here are all the flowers the girls wore in the

213

program—the star crosses, flutter-mills, bluebonnets, Indian paints. And buttercups. Buttercups more delicate than the shell of an egg or a porcelain cup or love. Flowers not meant to last.

L

I wonder what day it is. I wonder why it no longer matters. I wonder who's out there watching. And why?

I cannot remember Bob's face. Katie's is instantly before me. Hers, when she showed me her stomach, had the wary look of a wounded fox, like the one Christobel nursed.

Oh, dear God! Is there somebody watching? I cannot stand this much longer.

Diary!
Last night the wind rose. The wide, flat land around the building became an ocean of wind, tossing and threatening the barren schoolroom which groaned and creaked like a ship that had lost its moorings.

Sometime in the night, towards morning, the solitary sounds were interrupted by a clicking, like an animal's claws, on a wooden floor. I put my ear against the schoolhouse wall and listened. The clicking stopped, and then I heard a door open. And close. I leaned against the wall, shivering. As I stood there, I looked up through the window at the cold stars in the sky and . . . *Berl Monday's face was at the window*!

His torn ear was pressed against it as if he, too, were listening; his black, thick hair a pelt around his shoulders. For only a second, for the wink of an eye, his face was there, hanging against the blackness of the sky. Then it was gone.

I waited and I listened. All night I did not sleep.

But I am not crazy! *I have seen Berl Monday.*

Lucy Eliza Richards

May 1912

Dear Diary,

As the sun rose, I ran over to the schoolhouse. The slate board had been moved to just inside the door. It was inches away from my face when I threw open the door. On it he had written:

"I am watching you Miss Rishurds"

Well, I know that, Berl Monday, I thought shakily. I've known that for days. I picked up a piece of chalk and circled Berl's attempt at my name. Beneath it I wrote my name correctly. He should have known how to spell my name, I thought as I underlined "Richards." An eighth grader should have known that.

I'd find him, I decided, or better still, make it easy for him to find me. Gambol and I would ride out today; a horse and rider can be seen for miles on the prairie. But when I went out to Gambol's little shelter, he was gone! Strayed. I knew it as soon as I saw his empty water bucket. I had neglected him for days. Well, he'd find his way home. No need to worry about Gambol.

All day long I waited for Berl. While I waited, I tried not to think about Bob and Katie. Traitors! Both of them. Now I had only one sister. Katherine Ann Richards was no sister of mine. And where could I go? Not home. School was over, but I wouldn't go home. To grow old before my time. To live, like Aunt Catherine, in someone else's house, always the first to rise, the last to go to bed. To sleep in the smallest room. I would not be another Catherine.

The long day passed. The sun went down and still Berl did not come. The darkness, closing in, made me uneasy again. In the daytime Berl was no more than a former student—familiar, known, but at night I was not sure. I wondered where he slept. What he ate.

Finally, I fell asleep, but even sleeping I was alert to the sounds next door. After awhile I woke up and went to the window and sat, waiting for morning. Long before sunrise, the light came on. Gradually. At the corner of the schoolhouse, a black-limbed scrub oak lurched upward, like a dazed woman, into the vast sky. The poplar trees bent with the wind, coming together, pulling apart—a witches' coven.

Finally, it was broad daylight. Deliberately, I walked to the door and stepped outside. I did not look around. Opening the door of the schoolhouse, I looked only at the slate board. The words written there leapt out at me!

"My mama dyed Miss Richards"

Accused. Indicted. Oh, Berl, I am guilty. I confess it. I should have gone back that day. Your mother need not have died. Food. Wood for a fire. This was all she needed. I should have done that for her.

I looked at the words, and again I circled one: "dyed." Then the realization struck. Why, Berl means to kill me,

I thought, just as he killed Mr. Albright. Of course. He intends to kill me. He knows I am responsible for his mother's death. I am the guilty one. This was the reality of it. He was stalking me as he had stalked Olin Albright, waiting for me to stumble and fall as a drunken man would have done. Or, preferring an easier kill, would he come quietly while I slept?

The daylight was suddenly menacing. I stumbled back to the teacherage and closed the door.

Frantically, I pushed a school desk over to the door and tilted it just under the knob. I looked at the windows, dreading the glimpse of a ferret-like face that might be there. I flew to the trunk and pulled out the quilts that Mama had sent. I couldn't get the windows covered with them fast enough. I heard a strange, loud throbbing noise and, after a minute, knew it was the sound of my own heartbeat.

I willed myself to sit at the desk. I looked around the room, probing for places that might be vulnerable. Two high windows. A door. He could not come through the door. But if his head came through the window, or a foot. If I should look up and see a foot coming through the window!

I looked around the room for a weapon. The poker! I grabbed it from behind the stove. I looked back at the desk where I had been sitting. Now, it did not seem safe at all. I pushed the desk aside and moved the kitchen table close to the door. On top of it, I put both the desks. Then I sat on the bed.

Someone would come, I thought. Someone. Not Katie or Bob. Nor Josh. Josh would be in Tennessee by now. Who then? Christobel! If Christobel were home, she would come. Tomorrow. The day after. Or when it was dark, completely dark, I would slip out. I would slip out and make my way past Berl.

I was hungry. I remembered I had not eaten. I went to the pantry shelf. Dried beans. Flour. Canned tomatoes. The tomatoes made me think of H.H. It had been days since I had thought of him.

I opened the tomatoes and ate them. Behind the flour, I saw a box of tea. I opened it and dropped a handful of leaves into a pan. I picked up a pitcher to pour some water into the pan. The pitcher was empty.

I lay on the bed and waited for the night. While I waited, I looked at all the letters I had not opened. Seven were from Mama. Holding them, I knew the words she would have written, the "shoulds" and "should nots" and "musts" and "whys." There were five from Aunt Catherine. She would have written about her garden: her pole beans and sweet peas, her early corn in tassel and silk.

There was one from Christobel. I opened it, but not until the end of the letter could I focus on what she said:

. . . and Petey. It is as if the hurt and the betrayal he felt when he was ostracized by his classmates had shaped a new quality in him. He has always been gentle and easy, but now there is a something more. He is so sure now, so certain of himself. He never wavers. Well, my description does not do him justice. You will just have to see for yourself.

In the meantime, he sends his love, and I send mine.

Christobel

While I read that last part again and again, I fell asleep and dreamed I held a strong hand in mine as I walked beside a lake with choppy waves tipped by white caps. Keats, I thought, when I woke up.

A moan! I realized I had been awakened by a moan. Not the schoolhouse. The sound came from a human being. I heard it again. More faintly. Then I heard my name. Someone had called my name. It was a trick. I'd not go outside. Berl was crafty, but I could be too. Outside, in the daylight, I'd be an easy prey.

I tiptoed to the door and listened. Nothing. I took one of the desks off the table and pushed it under the window. I stood on the desk and pulled aside a corner of the quilt, afraid of the face that might be just outside.

The figure of a woman lay near the merry-go-round. Her feet were under it, her brown clothes jumbled, as if tossed there, like a tumbleweed.

Mrs. Dawson. It was Mrs. Dawson!

Hastily, I pulled the fortress, piece by piece, away from the door. I ran outside, across the schoolyard, and fell to my knees beside the woman.

"Mrs. Dawson, what is it? What is it? What's the matter?"

She opened her eyes. "Miss Richards, kin you help me? I'm . . . Giles's gone . . ." A spasm of pain crossed her face. Beads of perspiration broke out on her forehead. She moaned again. "I'm afraid that baby's comin'. Oh, I know it's comin'."

"I've got to get you inside. Can you sit up? Can you walk?"

I slipped my arm behind her back and pulled her forward.

She shook her head. "Can't walk now. It's too late."

"Help," I cried. "Oh, somebody help us. Oh, please, somebody!"

I ran back inside the teacherage and jerked the quilts from the windows. Outside again, I knelt by Mrs. Dawson's side. I put one quilt under her head and covered her with the other, all the while whispering, "Somebody's got to help us! Please. Oh, dear, God! We've got to have some help."

I felt a hand on my shoulder. Heavy. Dirty. The nails torn and jagged. I looked up. Berl Monday, his face expressionless, stood there, looking down at me!

Reeling, I sat back on my heels. I waited. Finally, "You haven't learned to spell," I said.

"No, but I can help you. Why you know I can help you," he said. "Just say what you want, Miss Richards. What do you want me to do? Say it!"

I looked at Mrs. Dawson. Her lip was bleeding a little. Her hair was down around her shoulders. Pretty, even now.

"I don't know what to do," I said, finding my voice again, "but let's get her inside. We've got to do that."

Berl knelt and swung her up in his arms as easy as anything.

I ran ahead of him. Inside, I smoothed out the bed and plumped the pillows. As he came through the door another spasm caught her, taking her whole body in a vise-like grip, a grip so strong that Berl had to stand there, with her in his arms, until it passed. Then he laid her gently on the bed.

I remembered whispered tales of childbirth. "We need lots of hot water," I said.

Berl was gone before the words were out of my mouth. I threw some wood in the stove and lit the fire. I put on a washtub, ready for the water that Berl had begun to carry in, bucket after bucket.

Mrs. Dawson lay quietly now, a trampled, exhausted thing. I went to the bed and touched her forehead. "Mrs. Dawson, where is Mr. Dawson?"

"Gone to get Miz Constable," she said. "But that baby's not gonna o-o-o-o-o-h!" The last word became a hard groan. She snatched up my hand and held it.

"Berl, put some water in the basin, and scrub your hands," I said. "After that, bring more towels from my trunk, and . . ."

I did not have time to finish. Suddenly, Mrs. Dawson pulled herself up on her elbows, emitting a series of swift, guttural sounds. Then she fell back, tossing, moaning, sobbing.

I squeezed her hand. "Easy, easy," I whispered. "We're here. We'll help you."

One of her hands, puffy and reddened, crept up over her huge stomach, restlessly caressing it, caressing her breasts that had already begun to leak.

"That baby's comin'. Oh, it's comin'. Dear God, help me. It's comin'."

"Berl, help her. Hold her. Let her hold onto your hand!"

Going to the foot of the bed, I drew aside the quilt. Her dress was pulled above her waist. A stream of water, warm and buoyant, poured from between her legs.

"Ugh, ugh." The sounds she made were inhuman. Her hand traced a haphazard pattern, skittering across her heaving belly like a frightened mouse. Her legs flew apart, revealing bloody thighs.

Without thinking or knowing how I knew, I eased my hands between her legs, and there! I felt the crown of the baby's head! Now the head was out! In my hands! I was holding the baby's head! It was wet and warm. Another moan. The baby was coming; I took it in my hands. Its head rested in the palm of my hand, its body along the length of my arm. Such a little thing! It lay there, gasping soundlessly, sucking oxygen from the air. "Here," Berl said, moving to my side. He took the baby, turning it gently, upside down. The baby cried. A tough, strong cry that shook the room.

"It's a girl, Mrs. Dawson," I said. "You have a baby girl."

Mrs. Dawson opened her eyes. "Well, I never. A girl. I never believed it would happen. I never really thought it!" Her eyes were filled with wonder; I thought of Katie's eyes at Christmas.

Berl tied off the cord and cut it. He worked quickly, as if he had done this a hundred times. I wondered how he knew, how I had known. Was this a knowledge we all shared? Something as arcane and mysterious as life itself?

While Berl tended the baby, I changed the bed linens and found a clean gown for Mrs. Dawson. Then I wrapped the baby in a soft, blue linen towel. I stepped to the bed to lay her beside her mother, but Mabel Dawson's eyes were closed. I couldn't tell if she was asleep.

I motioned to Berl to open the door and, holding the baby, tiptoed outside. Berl eased the door shut behind us, and we sat on the steps in the warm sunshine.

"Look! Just look at that!" Berl whispered.

A small foot had found its way through the towel. Together, we examined the toes, so little I had to lean over to see them clearly. I counted them. I tucked the foot back inside the towel and peered at her face. Her eyelids were the thinnest things I had ever seen. She opened her eyes and stared at me. A small fist, thrust outward, fell, touching Berl's hand. Berl carefully put his fore-finger into the small hand. The baby looked solemnly at me and curled her hand around Berl's finger. "Well," he said, exhaling a long sigh.

"Berl, I thought you were going . . . I was afraid you would . . . " It was hard to tell him that only a little while ago, I had thought he was going to kill me. I thought about the words he had written on the slate board.

"Why were you watching me? Why were you hiding?" I asked.

"Mama said the sheriff would be looking for me. I knew that being a stickler for the law, and a teacher and all, you'd turn me in."

"But you were watching me," I said. "Why?"

"After Mr. Arnold shot yore dog, after he left, somebody had to see to you."

"I am watching *over* you," the words had meant, not "I am watching you."

Unexpected tears filled my eyes.

"Oh, Berl! Oh, Berl, you don't know, you just don't know," but seeing his face, his bewildered expression, "how glad I was to see you," I finished lamely.

I thought about telling him the sheriff was not looking for him, or for anybody. Then I started to ask him if he had killed Mr. Albright. But now, the baby was asleep. I tiptoed inside and put her in her mother's arms.

When I came outside again, Berl was gone.

I sat down on the steps, leaned my head against the door, and looked up at the sky. It was a nice day for a baby to come. I wondered who would be there for Katie when her time came. Probably all the doctors in the county. She would never be poor. But she would have all those Sunday afternoons in the parlor, Sunday after Sunday with the Sully women. I wondered what Bob was thinking that very minute. I wondered if he ever thought of me, and I realized I hadn't the faintest idea. All those months I had never known what he thought.

The wind lifted for a minute, setting the poplar leaves into a soft frenzy of rustling, bringing a smell of wild horsemint. Josh. He'd be glad about the baby. I closed my eyes and went to sleep. The first sound sleep I'd had in days.

May 14, 1912
The Teacherage

Dear Mama,

At first, I thought I'd die when Katie ran away and married Bob. And it's not all right yet, between Katie and me. But I hope, I believe, that someday it might be. The Board of Trustees asked me back for another year; they offered me a raise in pay and said they'd build me a real house. I told them I'd like to think about it for awhile.

Now I'm coming home. Tell Uncle Jerry I'm looking forward to some tomatoes and green beans from the garden, and Mama, please bake me a cake with lemon filling.

I love you.

Lucy

May 14, 1912
The Teacherage

Dear Aunt Catherine,

Remember how Papa used to talk about a sea change when he knew that business would be better soon. Or his arthritis. That's how I feel now. It's as if in some part of me there's been a reversal, an imperceptible shifting, like a swirl in a current at the bottom of the sea. I don't know why, or how it came about, but it has something to do with the Dawson's baby and Berl Monday, who watched over me, and Petey's music.

I guess Katie did what she thought she had to do. And Bob, too.

For now, it's good to know that you will be at the station, waiting when I get home.

Love,
Lucy

May 16, 1912
The Teacherage

Dear Josh,

Mabel Dawson's baby came. Berl Monday and I delivered it. Mrs. Dawson said the baby looked just like me and, in the next breath, "Guess what we're going to call her."

Waiting for her to say my name (after all, I had helped bring the baby into the world), I said, "Oh, Mrs. Dawson, what?"

"Fosteen," she said triumphantly. "Now isn't that a purty name?" Knowing how you would have laughed at my surprise, I could hardly keep from laughing myself.

I wish you could have been here the day Fosteen was born. Christobel and Petey arrived first in Cable's Hupmobile, with Mr. Dawson riding the running board.

Mr. Dawson looked down at his newborn baby, asleep in his wife's arms. For a minute he stood there, pulling at his beard. Then he said, "I wanted a boy."

Christobel said, "Well, you'll take a girl, Giles Dawson, and be glad about it."

Christobel bustled about, bathing the baby and settling her in the crib that she had brought. Cable and
Ruby came a little later, driving the Dawson's wagon. (I
had not known Ruby was a widow with two little ones of
her own until she handed Mrs. Dawson a box of clothes
her own babies had outgrown.) Then Cable opened a jug
of wine, and we toasted the baby and the baby's mother
and daddy.

Josh, I've been thinking about a lot of things these past
few days. I know you had to shoot H.H., and I know how
you hated doing it. You did that for me, and a lot more.
You taught me to laugh at things, and you taught me to
love John Keats' poems. Christobel said, "Josh Arnold
will take the woman he loves up the mountain." I am beginning to understand all that she meant by that.

Your friend,

Lucy

May 18, 1912
On the Texas and Pacific

Dear Diary,

I'm on my way home. In an hour or so I'll see all those
dear faces again, all but Katie's.

So much to think about. To remember. That last time
in the schoolhouse yard. Petey's smile when he got out of
the car. His grin, as without a word, he walked right into
the schoolhouse and began to play. Then all those soft,
sweet lullabies that came floating out the windows.
Some I'd known all my life, and some I'd never heard.
Berl had drifted off somewhere, but when he heard the
music, he reappeared out by the merry-go-round, keep-

ing his distance, as if he was not sure of his welcome. Cable and Ruby arrived a little later in the Constable wagon. For a while we just listened to the baby's music. Then Petey stopped playing a few minutes as if to say by the silence, "Now I've played for the baby." He began again, and, at first, the music was angry, filled with discord and rumbling, with harsh notes that jarred. He's playing that for me, I thought. That's how I've felt these past weeks. But then, gradually, the music became tranquil and rich, the cadences peaceful. Then, he added a beat to the melody he was playing. Light. Varying it. Irresistible. Cable took Ruby's hand and led her out onto the schoolground. They began to dance. Petey must have seen them, for then he played a rollicking two-step. When Christobel came outside, Cable beckoned to her to join them, and seeing Berl standing out by the merry-go-round, she two-stepped over and pulled him into the circle. Then Ruby grabbed Mr. Dawson, who was grinning toothlessly. "Come on, Daddy Dawson, you got to dance this one!" she cried.

I sat on the steps and watched Christobel, who loves Mr. Sully, and Berl who has nobody, and Mr. Dawson, who had wanted a boy, watched them dancing, and I said to myself, "Lucy, you could sit here on these steps forever, waiting for things to be right."

And I got up and walked out to where the dancing was.

Lucy